HONOR-BOUND WITCH

MISS MATCHED MIDLIFE DATING AGENCY

BOOK TWO

DEANNA CHASE

Bayou Moon Press, LLC

www.deannachase.com

Printed in the United States of America

ABOUT THIS BOOK

A Paranormal Women's Fiction Novel.

Welcome to Miss Matched Midlife Dating Agency, where Marion Matched is ready to help you find your soul mate.

With her new dating agency business starting to take off in Premonition Pointe, Marion Matched is busier than ever. Between yoga classes, her budding romance, and the ghost who won't stop haunting her, Marian can't seem to find time to get her hair colored and her upper lipped waxed for the upcoming wedding of her two favorite clients. Whoever said women should grow older gracefully never had to deal with patchy gray roots or whiskers that are stiff enough to cut someone. But all of her grooming worries vanish when the bride suddenly goes AWOL. Now Marion finds herself in the middle of literal witch hunt with the bride's surly brother-in-law to be, while a bad actor seems to be sabotaging the lives of her friends and family. With everything falling apart around her, Marion will need all the help she can get from the Premonition Pointe coven, her resident ghost, and an untrustworthy new acquaintance to find her friend before she disappears forever.

CHAPTER 1

"There you are!" Lennon Love grabbed my hand and tugged, pulling me toward the stage. The steady strum of base reverberated through the club as the almost-naked men on stage gyrated to the music, making the women in the audience scream their approval.

"Lennon, I—"

"It's your time to shine, Marion!" she yelled over the music as a grin spread across her face. We were at *Abs, Buns, and Guns* watching a male strip show for her bachelorette party. It most definitely wasn't my time to shine. I was just there to support her.

I glanced over my shoulder at Hollister Crooner. The tall, dark-haired man was standing by the bar with his hands shoved in his pockets, frowning at me. I couldn't exactly blame him. He'd come to *Abs, Buns, and Guns* just to tell me that his brother's fiancée, Kiera Vincent, was missing.

Kiera was a former client of mine who'd changed her name after leaving an abusive relationship. I was the only one who knew her real full name was Desiree Ciaràn Hopkins.

Everyone else knew her as Kiera Vincent. If she was missing, there was a good chance her ex-boyfriend had found her. My heart started to thunder against my breastbone, and the desire to bolt and head back over to Hollister had me turning in his direction.

"There she is," the emcee said into the mic. "Marion Matched, the woman who matched Lennon and Bodhi, making this night possible. Come on up here, Marion. We have a surprise for you."

"I can't—" I started, shaking my head.

"Of course you can." Lennon gave me a gentle push, mischief shining in her amused eyes. "Go on, Marion. There's no way I'm going to let you miss this."

I opened my mouth to protest again. Hollister was waiting, and I had to do whatever I could to help him find his future sister-in-law. But before I could speak, two pairs of strong hands lifted me up by my armpits and swept me up onto the stage.

The crowd went wild. Women stood, hooting and hollering, shouting their approval.

I was placed in a chair in the middle of the stage while oiled men in skimpy underwear surrounded me.

Lennon threw her head back and laughed as one proceeded to shake his tush in my face and then acted as if he were grinding in my lap. On any other day, I'd have been howling with laughter, caught up in the ridiculousness of it all. But today, all I could do was grit my teeth and bear it. I couldn't just jump up and run off the stage. Not without making a scene and having to stop to explain why I was refusing the lap dance that Lennon had obviously orchestrated.

Explaining anything about Kiera to a crowd could *not* happen. It was too dangerous. Instead, I decided it was best to wait it out and then make my excuses and find Iris, who was supposed to be meeting me outside to leave with Hollister.

"Yassss!" Celia, the ghost who worked for me, cried. She was floating in front of the man pretending to grind against me, swinging an invisible rope as she acted as if she were trying to lasso him. "Now this is what I call a party!"

All the women at the bachelorette party were on their feet. Some of them waved dollar bills and demanded that they were next. I spotted my friend Tandy up on a chair, waving her cash at us. My aunt Lucy was beside her, gyrating around, and I wondered briefly if she was going to throw a hip out of joint. My aunt caught my eye and grinned.

I gave Lucy a tight smile while trying to keep an eye on Hollister and impatiently waiting for my chance to bolt from the stage.

"Come on, Marion!" Lennon called. "Show us your moves!"

"Moves?" I muttered. "What moves?"

The muscled man, who'd shown me more of his backside than ought to be legal, held his hand out to me, inviting me to my feet.

I let him tug me up out of the chair and then stood there while a second man danced behind me with his hands on my hips and a third dropped it like it was hot in front of me, bouncing up and down with his head right at my crotch.

Good goddess, I thought. *When will this end?*

And then I had to just chuckle, because damn. Was I so old that I couldn't appreciate the over-the-top entertainment that was clearly riling up the rest of the crowd? If it hadn't been for Hollister waiting for me, I hoped I'd have been able to let my hair down and have a little fun at least.

"Swing your hips, Marion," The dancer behind me said into my ear. "Let loose a little."

Lennon was behind the dancer who was right in front of me, letting the dancer place her hands on his chest, encouraging her to get her fill of his muscles. He was grinning, clearly enjoying her shrieks of mock protest. When he caught me watching him, he winked and said, "It's all in good fun."

"Sure," I said and firmly kept my hands to myself as I bent my knees and swayed my hips in time to the music. Just as my body started to relax and get into the rhythm, the song ended and the dancer in front of me grabbed my hand.

I started to pull it back, ready to protest whatever else they had in store for me, but the dancer bent and kissed the back of my hand.

"Thanks for being a good sport," he said. And that's when everything went haywire.

The lights went out, and we were plunged into complete darkness while a loud crash sounded from across the bar.

A ring of fire illuminated the club right where I'd last seen Hollister, followed by a chorus of shrieks as the crowd jumped away from the flames. Just as soon as the fire appeared, it vanished and a crackle of magic lit up the room like a bolt of lightning.

"Hollister!" I cried out, terrified that he'd been targeted. It was just too much of a coincidence that he'd shown up to tell me Kiera was missing, and then suddenly fire and magic were crackling right where he'd been standing.

Silence followed, and then everyone started talking at once.

I blinked rapidly, silently pleading for my eyes to adjust in the darkness as I crab-walked forward, my hands on the stage so that I wouldn't walk right off the edge. I had to get to Hollister and make sure he was okay.

Just as I reached the edge of the stage, there was a loud electric zapping sound, followed by the flicker of lights. All the women stood around staring up at the ceiling until the light stabilized, and then they started chattering again.

I glanced once at Lennon, who was already talking to the two dancers who'd sandwiched me on stage. There was a worried expression on her face as she gestured around the club, clearly upset by the turn of events, but they appeared to be soothing her concerns.

"It wasn't that great of a lap dance," Celia said, sounding annoyed as she came to stand next to me on the stage. "Danny would have done it better."

"I'm sure he would have," I said absently as I hopped down onto the main floor and made a beeline for the bar where I'd last seen Hollister.

"Can you imagine Danny with his hands all up in my business—"

"No offense, Celia, but now isn't the time," I said, exasperated. Normally Celia was pretty entertaining, but in that moment, I didn't need to hear about her fantasies.

"It's never the time, Marion," she said, sounding annoyed. "Like last week when I tried to tell you about that blow job—"

Her words faded away as I finally pushed my way through the crowd and stared down at the wooden floor right where I'd last seen Hollister. In his place was a circle burned into the floor, and right in the middle there was a dagger lodged into the hardwood, holding a thick piece of parchment in place.

"What the fresh hell is this?" asked Tandy, my best friend, coming to a stop beside me. She reached down to grab the dagger, but a sharp stab of magic zapped her fingers, sending a bolt of electricity straight up her arm. She yelped and jumped back, cradling her arm to her chest. "That thing tried to kill me."

The crowd took a collective step back, all of them whispering frantically, trying to figure out what was going on.

"Mother effer," I mustered and reached for her. "Are you okay?"

She tried to roll her shoulder and winced. "That hurt like a son of a bitch. But I'm probably not dying."

I gently squeezed her good arm in sympathy, trying to keep my rage in check. Whoever had done this had just hurt my best friend with their booby trap.

Lennon ran over, looking frazzled as she looked from me to the circle and then at her new boss. Lennon had just signed a deal to star in Tandy's next television project. "Holy shit, Marion, has someone been cursed *again*?"

"I don't know," I said honestly. "All I know is that a man has gone missing and in his place is this… note? Message? I don't know."

"A man has gone missing?" she parroted. "Who?"

"Hollister. He's— You know what? Never mind. He came here to ask for my help, and now he's gone." I bent down to eye the note, trying to read it without touching anything. I wasn't looking to be zapped like Tandy had been. But if anything was written on the parchment, it must've been on the other side. I couldn't make out anything except a logo, or maybe a family crest, that was in the shape of a pentagon with the letter *C* stylized in the center.

"I recognize that crest," Celia said, eyeing the parchment.

"You do?" I asked the ghost in astonishment. "How?"

"It's the same one that was on a building that used to be next to the coffee shop I frequented in my neighborhood in LA. It was a New Age business, devoted to spells and potions. Crooner's Cauldron, I think."

Crooner? As in Hollister Crooner? What the hell kind of

game was Hollister playing? I straightened, ready to search the club high and low for the man, when a woman who'd clearly had too much to drink stumbled into me and sent me flying to the floor. I landed right next to the dagger in the middle of the circle, and to my surprise, a whisper of magic tickled my fingers. My hand seemingly moved on its own toward the dagger, and when I gripped the handle, there was no stab of magic. No pain. Just a feeling of rightness that the dagger was meant for me. I yanked it out of the floor and grabbed the note.

"Hey, how come it didn't zap you?" Tandy asked.

I stared up at her. "You make it sound like you *wanted* me to get zapped."

She gave me a sheepish look and then shook her head. "No, no. I'm just surprised is all. Was it a one-time booby trap?"

"Maybe." I turned the parchment over and read:

The party's over, Marion. Time to get to work. Find the black BMW X5.

"Pretentious prick," Celia said.

I glanced up to find her hovering over me, reading the note.

"You can say that again." It looked very much like Hollister had caused a scene and left a note only I could access because he was too impatient to just wait five minutes for the show to end. I got to my feet and glanced around at the crowd staring at me expectantly. "Celia," I whispered. "Quick. Go get the dancers and get them moving. I need this crowd distracted." There was no way I was going to explain who Hollister was or why he was there in Premonition Pointe. It was too dangerous for Kiera.

"On it," she said seriously and popped out of existence.

I waved the note in the air. "Looks like it's time to get the party started!" I yelled with forced exuberance. As if on cue,

7

the music started up, this time playing Bon Jovi's "Shot Through the Heart" as the dancers spilled out of the back, this time moving through the crowd, giving the women the attention they'd been dying for.

"Tandy," I said to my friend. "Do me a favor and keep these people dancing. Start the rumor that this was just all part of the show, you know, to keep things lively and add a bit of magic into the night."

She gave me a skeptical look, but when I asked again, she nodded. "Okay, but you're going to explain all of this later, right?"

"As much as I can," I said, squeezing her good arm again. "Thanks."

I quickly pulled Lennon aside and explained that everything was fine but that I had to go take care of something. As I was headed for the door, Iris suddenly appeared by my side.

"What the hell is going on?" she asked. "I was outside waiting, and when I couldn't find you, I ended up back in here with everyone standing around staring at you like you'd grown three heads."

"I might as well have," I said. "Follow me. We're about to get our answers." Then I headed out the door and straight toward the man who was leaning against his overpriced car, a cigarette in his hand as he glared at me.

CHAPTER 2

"hat in the hell did you think you were doing?" I demanded the moment Hollister was in earshot. I waved the note at him. "This stunt? This is exactly the kind of attention I was hoping to avoid."

Hollister's gaze flickered to Iris. "Who's this?"

"My friend and assistant. Believe me when I say, if there's anyone I can trust, it's her. Now explain what the hell just went down."

Iris glanced back and forth between us but thankfully kept quiet as she took in the scene playing out before her.

Hollister turned away from Iris, appearing to dismiss her, and his gaze bored into mine. "You were fucking around on stage. I needed to get your attention. It worked, right? You're here now."

I scoffed. "You certainly got my attention. And everyone else's in the room. Do you know what that kind of stunt could've caused? Don't you care about Kiera at all?"

He pushed off his car and stalked forward until we were toe to toe. "Why exactly do you think I'm here? The *only* thing I care about is finding Kiera. For some reason, she told Garrison you were the one to find if anything happened to her. Imagine my utter disgust to see you up on that stage right after I told you Kiera's missing. What was I supposed to do?"

"Not that!" I said through clenched teeth. "Listen, buddy, if I didn't need you to fill in some details, I'd already be trying to find her. But since I haven't been in touch with her in over a year, you're going to need to answer some questions. Understand?"

Iris sucked in an audible breath as her eyes widened, but she still didn't say anything as she watched us battle it out.

He scoffed. "I think you're the one who needs to answer some questions. Like how about you tell me why she said to find you if something happens to her."

I shook my head. "No way, Hollister. Not here and not until I'm satisfied that you're exactly who you say you are." The more this man talked, the more I was ready to deck him. I hadn't questioned him at first, but now… Who knew if he really was Garrison's brother? Maybe he was pretending to be someone he wasn't in order to track Kiera down.

"I don't have time for this." He pulled out his phone and tapped a screen. A moment later, he stepped up beside me and showed me the phone. His brother Garrison was on the line, staring at us, his face gaunt with dark circles under his eyes. "Gar," Hollister said. "Tell Marion what you told me." Hollister handed me the phone and took a step back.

"Garrison?" I asked, astonished to see the once-vibrant man looking like he'd lost twenty pounds and hadn't seen the sunlight in weeks. "What's going on? Are you sick?"

"Hollister didn't tell you?" he asked, his voice sounding stronger than he looked.

I shook my head, that pit of dread forming in my stomach

again. "He said Kiera is missing, but he didn't mention anything about you. Are you okay? Healthwise, I mean?"

"I'm doing as well as can be expected, I guess. It's cancer," he said quietly. "The treatments are almost done, but my immune system is weak and..." He swallowed hard. "I wanted to come to you myself, but Hollister insisted I stay here. He's afraid if I get sick..." Garrison's voice trailed off as he shook his head. "None of that is important now. I'll be fine. But Kiera left to pick up her wedding dress two days ago and never came home."

My immediate thought was that we had a runaway bride on our hands. Kiera had run before, so it was feasible she'd run again. But deep in my heart, I didn't believe it. I'd seen her and Garrison together. Hell, I'd been the one to set them up. Their connection had been instantaneous. They were the type of couple who just seemed to be able to see into each other's souls. I'd seen the love shining in her eyes when she looked at him. The idea that she'd run while he was going through cancer treatments was unthinkable.

I took a deep breath. "Okay. Tell me everything. Did anything unusual happen before she disappeared? Did you call the police and file a missing person's report? Does she have her phone? Have any of her friends heard from her? Is there anything different or unusual that's happened lately that might be a clue?"

Garrison closed his eyes and shook his head slowly. "No. No to all of that. Except her phone. She probably has that. Or at least she did before she left because she sent me a text about the flowers she'd picked out for our wedding."

My heart was breaking for him. This had to be killing him. I wanted to soothe him, to reassure him that everything would turn out okay, but I couldn't. I knew too much already. "Just to be sure, you're saying you didn't file a police report?" I asked, holding my breath as I waited for his answer.

"I… She left me very specific instructions to never do that. Do you think I should?" His eyes were glassy, and the poor man looked like he was on the verge of a nervous breakdown.

"No." It took everything in me not to shout the command. Garrison didn't need me yelling at him. "That's not a good idea. It's better if we handle this outside of the authorities."

He seemed to gather himself before he asked the question that he clearly didn't want to ask. "Was Kiera involved in anything… illegal?"

"No. Listen, I know Kiera didn't tell you anything about her past, and there's a very good reason for that," I said. "Right now, I just need you to trust me, okay? I'm going to do everything in my power to find her and bring her back to you. I promise."

His normally bright green eyes were dull, and he looked defeated as he nodded. "I trust Kiera. She told me to trust you, so that's what I'm going to do."

I nodded once. "I appreciate that. I'll get your number from your brother and keep you updated. If you can just email Hollister any details about what Kiera did the few days before she disappeared and what her routine was, that would be helpful."

"I'll do what I can," he said, his voice getting weaker by the second.

Hollister took the phone from me and told his brother to take a sleeping pill and get some rest. When Garrison protested, Hollister threatened to send over someone named Sally to make sure he wasn't overdoing anything. When Garrison shuddered and promised he'd get some rest, Hollister was placated and ended the call.

"Satisfied?" Hollister asked.

"I guess so. Let's go," I said.

"Go where?"

"You'll see. We have things to discuss. Just follow me in your car." I gestured to Iris to follow me as I stalked away toward my white SUV. I quickly pulled out my phone and sent a text to Tandy and my aunt Lucy to let them know I was leaving early. Then I turned to Iris. "Can you go back inside, grab the rest of the coven, and meet us at the coven circle?"

"Is this about the former client you texted me about?" she asked.

I nodded.

"Of course. I'm sure they'll want to do anything they can to help find your friend."

Gratitude washed over me. The fact that Iris was ready to help without demanding a full explanation was just one of the reasons why I loved her. I'd always had friends, but it wasn't until I met Tandy that I felt like I had a ride or die. And now Iris was one, too. I reached out and squeezed her hand. "Thank you. You have no idea how much this means to me. I'll explain as much as possible when we have the coven together."

"No thanks needed," Iris said, her eyes intense. "A friend of yours needs help. That's all I need to know." She gave me a quick hug and hurried back into the club.

As soon as the door closed behind Iris, I jumped into my SUV, thankful that the coven was there for me when I needed them. As I slid into the driver's seat, I realized I was still holding the dagger that Hollister had left in the club. As I set it on the seat beside me, magic flashed along the blade and then winked out just as fast.

I stared at it, wondering if it was left over from the spell Hollister had cast or if I'd somehow triggered it. The base of my spine started to tingle, and although I couldn't be sure, I thought I had my answer.

Ever since I'd lost my ability to see auras clearly when I saw two people who were right for each other, that tingle had been there. My fingers itched to touch the dagger again and see if anything changed. Slowly, I reached out and ran one finger over the engraved hilt.

Nothing.

Determined, I wrapped my hand around the handle and held the weapon up in the moonlight streaming through my window. The blade took on a blue shimmer, but there wasn't any spark of magic that I could see.

Sighing with a faint trace of disappointment, I placed the dagger back down on the seat and resigned myself to the idea that my only magic these days was a faint tingle at the base of my spine.

Some witch I'd turned out to be.

CHAPTER 3

"*Y*ou've taken me to a bluff overlooking the Pacific Ocean?" Hollister asked incredulously. "What were you planning to do? Push me over the edge?"

If only, I thought. But I wasn't in the business of offing people even if they did annoy the crap out of me. "No," I said with the practiced patience I used on my most difficult clients. "We're here because this is where the coven meets, and they are our best shot of finding Kiera quickly." I held out the dagger I'd grabbed from the seat of my car. "Here."

He glanced at the weapon and started to reach for it, but then his eyes narrowed and he shook his head. "No. It's yours now."

"What? No. I don't need something like this." I shoved it toward him. "This thing must have cost a fortune. As much as I don't appreciate how you used it back there at that club, I'm not one to keep things that don't belong to me."

"But it *does* belong to you." He nodded toward it. "Look at that blue tinge."

The moonlight was making it shimmer blue again. "What about it?"

"That only happens when a dagger like that claims someone. Whether I like it or not, that dagger is yours."

I frowned, eyeing the dagger as if looking for some clue that it might reveal. "I've never heard of that before."

He shrugged one shoulder. "You've probably never seen a dagger like that before."

"You're telling me this dagger is special in some way? What, is it forged from the mines of some magical mountain or something?"

"Something like that," he said vaguely and then shoved his hands in his pockets. "Just accept the dagger, Marion. Consider it payment for helping us find Kiera if you like."

I shook my head. "I would never take payment for helping Kiera. That's—"

He cut me off. "Fine. Consider it a gift. Either way, I'm not taking it back. And if you don't take it and it ends up in the wrong hands, then you'll be responsible."

"What could go wrong?" I asked, inspecting the dagger again. But then I quickly shook my head, remembering that the dagger had already been infused with magic. He was right. If it ended up in the wrong hands, who knew what could happen? I shoved it into the bag I was carrying as I said, "Never mind. That was a stupid question. Fine. I'll keep it."

He gave me a tight smile and then glanced out at the sea. "Is this where we're meeting your friends?"

"This way." I led him down the narrow path to the bluff that overlooked the churning waves and was surprised to see that Carly was already there. She had a salt circle ready to go and a ring of white pillar candles set up just inside the circle.

16

"How did you get here so soon?" I asked, a little confused. Was there a shortcut I didn't know about?

"I'd already left the party, so I had a shorter distance to go when Iris called." Carly stood and walked over to us, her sweater wrapped around her to stave off the evening chill. "Joy and Iris are on their way. Grace had a bit too much to drink at the bachelorette party and Hope's taking care of her because Owen is out of town. A drunk witch isn't really an asset when spellcasting. As for Gigi, she's unavailable because she helping Skyler try to win over an investor who might be interested in helping him open more locations of Sky's The Limit. Places like Aspen, Monterey, Martha's Vineyard. You know, areas that attract high-end clients who are interested in his designer clothing and our skin care line. Nothing major, just a few more stores."

I nodded, grateful that any of them could come on such short notice, and said, "I can imagine."

Carly held her hand out to Hollister. "Hi, I'm—"

"Carly Preston," he said, sounding awed. "I'd know you anywhere. My mom was a huge fan of yours. That movie, *Last Witch of Meadow Lake*, was one of her favorites. It gave her great comfort while she was going through her cancer treatments." He took her hand in both of his, holding on as if she'd just given him a treasured memory of his mother. "Thank you for that. At the end, that movie was one of the only things that gave her peace."

The smile slid off my friend's face, and her eyes turned glassy as she pulled him in to give him a hug. "I'm so sorry for your loss. I'm just grateful I was a part of something that touched so many people."

Hollister held on tight and then suddenly let her go and

took a step back. He cleared his throat. "I'm sorry. That… This isn't the time. Thank you for being so gracious."

"Of course," Carly said, giving him a sympathetic smile.

I felt a rush of love for my friend. Her kindness really knew no bounds.

The sound of voices came from behind us, and I turned to see Iris and Joy coming toward us.

"Thank you so much," I said, giving each of them a hug. "I'm sorry to interrupt your evenings… again." They'd just helped me try to find the source of a curse only a couple of weeks ago.

"Don't worry about it," Joy said, frowning at me. "Iris said there's a person missing. What happened? Who is it?"

Hollister glanced at me and then at Joy and Iris. "It's my soon to be sister-in-law. She went missing two days ago, and she told my brother that if anything ever happened to her to never call the authorities. He had to call Marion. My brother isn't well enough to travel, so here I am."

Iris studied Hollister and then turned to me. "Is there a good reason to not call the authorities?"

"Yes," I said without hesitation.

The former mayor of Premonition Pointe was well aware that not all authority figures were trustworthy. She nodded once and then took a deep breath. "Okay. Then let's get started. Do you have a picture of her?"

Hollister fished a picture out of his wallet and tried to hand it to Iris, but Joy stepped up and took it.

"She's lovely," Joy said, gazing down at what looked like an engagement photo of both Kiera and Garrison.

"She is," Hollister said, all traces of irritation and snark gone from his tone. "My brother…" He swallowed hard. "He needs her."

I nodded and reached out to squeeze his hand. When our

18

fingers touched, that tingle at the base of my spine flared to life again. Hollister glanced over, and a small wrinkle creased his forehead as he studied me.

I gave him a quick sympathetic smile before dropping his hand and shoving mine in my pocket.

"Joy?" Carly asked tentatively. "Is everything all right?"

I turned to the tall blonde still holding the picture. Her eyes were wide but unseeing as she gazed out at the sea. Her body was stiff as if she were in a trance, her hair flowing out behind her in the sea breeze.

"What's happening?" Hollister asked me.

I shook my head. I had my suspicions, but I wasn't going to voice them. If I was correct and Joy was having a vision, I wasn't going to do anything to interrupt it.

Carly and Iris moved to either side behind Joy, leaving me standing in front of her. The three of us made a small circle around her, and I knew that was for protection. If Joy was in a trance, the coven members were doing their part to make sure she was safe.

Hollister opened his mouth to speak again, but I held my hand up, stopping him. He promptly closed his mouth but shifted his feet, clearly out of patience. As long as he didn't pull another stunt like he had back at the club, I didn't care how he felt about this situation. He'd come to me for help, and this was what I had to offer.

Joy let out a small gasp and pressed her free hand to her mouth as her eyes finally came into focus. "She was headed north on 101 when she went missing, about forty-five miles south of here."

"What?" Hollister and I said at the exact same time.

Hollister turned to me with accusation in his eyes. "Was she coming here? To see you?"

"I have no idea," I said, shaking my head. "I haven't heard from Kiera in over a year. Not since she and your brother got engaged."

He narrowed his eyes. "I don't think I believe you."

Okay, this guy was really starting to get on my last nerve. "I don't really care what you believe. What I care about is what else Joy saw."

Iris cleared her throat. Always the diplomat, she said, "We're all here to find Kiera, right? Why don't we just hear Joy out and then go from there?"

Hollister closed his eyes for a moment, rolling his shoulders as he visibly tried to calm himself. "Yeah. Okay. Is Joy some sort of seer or something?"

"She can sometimes see visions when touching pictures," Carly said, placing a soft hand on Joy's arm. "That's how she helped me find my niece when she was abducted not that long ago."

"I see," Hollister said, looking at Joy with renewed interest. He ran a hand through his messy curls and asked, "What else did you see?"

Joy stared down at the picture and then paced the small area as she began to speak. "She was in a blue car. It looked like a Honda emblem. Music was playing, the window was down, and she was singing along to a Bruno Mars song. The one about counting on your friends. At first glance, it appeared she was enjoying the drive and the sunny day, but there was a sadness about her and tears in her eyes."

I frowned. Kiera wasn't one to show a lot of emotion, but that didn't mean she didn't let her guard down when she was alone.

"She drives a blue Honda Accord," Hollister said quietly.

Nodding, Joy continued. "She stopped at a beach area, got a

snack from a food truck in the parking lot, and then took a short walk on the beach. After dipping her toes into the ocean, she sat on a picnic bench for about forty-five minutes. She was looking around and appeared to be waiting for someone. After checking her watch multiple times, she finally headed back to her car. There was a black SUV parked next to her. It looked like she hesitated for a moment, but then she stiffened her spine and climbed back into her car. When she pulled out of the parking lot, she headed north again and the SUV followed her."

I sucked in a sharp breath. "She always said black SUVs made her nervous. She always thought they were following her, but she'd tried to take steps to overcome her fear. How could she not when black SUVs are everywhere all over the roads?"

"She was right to be nervous," Joy said, her tone ominous. "Because about ten miles up the road when no one else was around, that SUV forced her off the road into a ditch. And that's when goons from the SUV jumped out, yanked her from her car, stuffed her in the back of the SUV, and then drove off without anyone seeing a thing." Joy sat down on one of the logs, holding her head in her hands. "She was so scared. I can feel the fear that was rippling through her."

"Where did they take her?" Hollister asked, determination in his tone.

Joy shook her head. "I don't know for sure. I didn't see any signs in that area. The beach was just a turnout. But the food truck had a stylized J on the side, and they were serving sandwiches."

"That's not a lot to go on," Hollister said, sounding frustrated.

"I know." Joy glanced up at him. "But it's all I've got."

I moved to sit next to Joy and wrapped an arm around her shoulders. "It's a lot more than we had five minutes ago."

Hollister walked over to stand right in front of me. "I think it's time you tell me everything you know."

A war raged inside of me. Kiera had sworn me to silence. Made me promise to keep everything she'd told me to myself. She didn't want anyone else to be targeted by her ex. I understood her intentions, but now that the worst had happened, I was going to have to choose people I trusted to help me find her. Because there was no way I could do it on my own.

I took a deep breath and nodded. I trusted the coven members. Would trust them with my life. The only question was if I could trust Hollister. After the phone call with his brother, it was clear that Hollister would do anything for Garrison. Would he get involved in this and leave Garrison out of it? Make sure that Garrison didn't become a target? There was only one way to find out.

"I'll tell you, but in order to keep Garrison safe, you can't tell him anything I reveal to you. You have to promise that this is just between us," I said.

He glanced at the coven members. "But you will tell them?"

I nodded. "I'll give them the choice. The information I have could put all of you in danger if I tell you."

"I'm in," Joy said immediately. She stood from the log and straightened her shoulders. "No sister left behind. I can't just forget what I saw."

"If she's important to you," Iris added, "then I'm in, too. A friend of yours is a friend of mine."

Carly nodded her agreement. "After what happened to Harlow, I can't just sit back and let this happen to anyone else. If I can be of any help, I'm in."

I turned to Hollister. "The people Kiera ran from are dangerous. There's a reason she's never told anyone but me about her past. Are you sure you want the details? Knowing what I'm about to tell you could put your life in danger."

"I'm sure," he said with a curt nod.

It was no surprise that he'd been willing to jump in with both feet. From what I'd gathered about Hollister Crooner, he wasn't a man who was willing to back down when he wanted something.

"Okay." I took a seat on one of the logs in the coven circle and then gestured for everyone else to do the same. Once they were all sitting, I said, "I met Kiera the night she finally made the break from her ex. It was by pure chance, but I happened to be at the right place at the right time to help her finally attain her freedom. But if she were to tell it, she'd say I was in the wrong place at the wrong time. And she has always maintained that if her ex-boyfriend ever found out that I was the one who helped her, then he'd come after me."

"Who's her ex?" Hollister asked, just as impatient as he'd been back at the club.

"I don't know," I said. "She was careful to never tell me that part. All I know is that he works in law enforcement. And she believes that if she ever reports him, he's high enough in the chain of command that not only will he not be brought to justice, but he'd find a way to pin something on her and she'd be the one who would wind up in jail. She always believed her only option was to just disappear because anything less would mean she'd lose her freedom."

Hollister frowned. "How does knowing that put us in danger?"

"Kiera said that two people in her past who had tried to help her just disappeared. Their families were lied to and their

23

cases were quietly closed without any real investigation." I pressed a hand to my heart to keep it from beating right out of my chest. "The only reason Kiera told me anything is because I found her after she'd sprained an ankle while climbing out of a bathroom window in a small town in Utah."

"Utah?" Carly asked. "What were you doing there?"

I had lived in LA prior to moving to Premonition Pointe, so it was a fair question. "I was on my way home from a trip to Bryce and Zion with a couple of friends from college. I'd met them there and was driving back."

"What was Kiera doing in Utah?" Hollister asked.

"The same thing, I think. She didn't live there, but she never did tell me why she and her boyfriend were in that town. I only know she'd had enough and was ready to run. She said she didn't know anyone in town and figured that was the best place to hop on a bus to nowhere. She had some money and a fake ID she'd picked up somewhere along the way sewn into the lining of her jacket, and she had a large diamond ring and tennis bracelet to pawn. Nothing else. Not a change of clothes or even a phone. Her boyfriend wouldn't let her have one."

"No phone," Iris said almost to herself and shook her head. "Classic sign of abuse."

I nodded. "Right. Anyway, when I insisted on helping her, she was so shaken up and scared since she was unable to walk that she accepted. Once we were in my car, I tried to take her to a healer, but she broke down and told me I had to just drop her off at a bus station so that she could leave town. She said it wasn't safe. I refused, of course, because she was obviously in pain and I wasn't going to leave someone in a vulnerable position like that, so I ended up taking her all the way back to LA. Once we were home, I called in a healer to do a house call."

"She rode with a stranger all the way from Utah to LA?" Carly asked, concern etched all over her lovely features.

"Yes," I said. "She told me later that her only choice was either having her boyfriend find out she was trying to escape or getting in my car. My car seemed safer."

"No doubt," Joy said. "How many years has it been?"

"Six. She stayed with me for about six months. During that time, she started an online business as a graphic designer. It's easy to be anonymous online. She started making enough money that she got her own apartment. She hired a lawyer who helped her legally change her name and keep it out of public records. We stayed in touch, and two years ago she let me set her up with Garrison. She did everything she could to get away from her ex and keep her former identity secret. How he found her now is a mystery, but there's no doubt in my mind that he's behind her abduction. It's what she's been afraid of since the moment she jumped out of that window."

Carly's hands had balled into fists, and her lips were twisted into a scowl. "That piece of shit. We won't let him get away with this."

"No, we won't," I agreed. Kiera was the kindest, most thoughtful person I'd ever met. She deserved only the best in the world. I'd go to the ends of the earth to find her and put her egotistical, psychotic ex in his place. Even if that place was six feet under.

"Let me get this straight," Hollister said. "She hasn't told anyone this other than you, no one, not even Garrison, because she's afraid her ex will go after them next?"

"Yes," I said.

He scoffed. "Who the hell is her ex? Someone from the mafia? Or a drug kingpin from Central America whose found his way into our law enforcement?"

I shrugged. "Maybe? Kiera said she knew things that she shouldn't know and that her ex would do anything to find her. She thought that after so many years, maybe he'd given up." Tears stung my eyes as I tried to push all the awful images of what Kiera was enduring at that very moment from my mind. "Obviously he didn't. Now it's up to us to find her."

"Without law enforcement," Hollister said. "But what if I know someone I trust?"

"It's too dangerous," I said. "Not without knowing who her ex is. Law enforcement protects their own."

Hollister didn't seem convinced, but after a few seconds, he gave me a curt nod. "All right. How do we find out who her ex is?"

I glanced around at the coven.

Iris lifted her head. "We have our ways, but it's going to take a few days."

Hollister raised one skeptical eyebrow.

"You can doubt us all you want, but this isn't our first rodeo when it comes to dealing with powerful forces." Iris turned to the two other coven members. "Can you meet tomorrow? Maybe Grace, Hope, and Gigi will be available, too."

Joy and Carly nodded.

"In the meantime," I said, "Joy, if you can write down any identifying markers from your vision, Hollister and I can try to find the area where Kiera was taken. See if there are any clues in her car. That kind of thing."

"Sure." Joy rummaged around in her purse and came up with a piece of paper and a pen. After jotting some notes down, she handed it to me. Then she turned to Hollister. "Do you have anything of Kiera's we can use to try finding spell?"

"Like what?" he asked.

"Something that's important to her or that she usually keeps on her person," I said.

"If she keeps it on her person, why would I have it?" he asked, clearly annoyed.

"That's just one of the things," Carly said patiently. "It can be anything that is infused with her essence."

"I don't," he said. "But Garrison will have something. I could have him overnight it."

"He could," Iris said. "But it won't get here tomorrow. It's faster if someone goes and gets it."

Hollister blew out a breath. "I could go back there, but I'd rather start looking for Kiera."

"As much as I want to go look for her right this minute," I said, "I think it's best if we wait until the sun comes up. Finding anything in the dark, especially on the coast, is going to be impossible."

Hollister gritted his teeth. He clearly wasn't fond of the plan, but what other choices did he have? "I'll take a look on my way back, see if I can locate her car. I'll let you know if I find anything."

It was as good a plan as any. I nodded and then turned to my friends. "You'll do a finding spell once you have something of Kiera's and ask Angela to keep an ear out?"

Joy nodded. Angela was Hope's mother. She could hear people's thoughts, and while that was often overwhelming to her, she didn't hesitate when someone was in trouble. Joy placed her hand on Hollister's sleeve. "If you have any more recent pictures of Kiera, bring those, too. I'll keep trying for more visions."

"Yeah, okay." Hollister programmed my number into his phone and then strode off back to the road.

I stood with the rest of the coven members, staring out at

27

the sea. Without speaking, the three of them joined hands, and then Iris reached for mine.

Carly started to sing the Pagan song "We Do Not Die." Her voice was low, haunting, and full of beauty. That tingle at the base of my spine was back, and somehow, their voices managed to fill me with hope that one way or another, we'd find Kiera before it was too late.

CHAPTER 4

*M*y house was dark and silent as I slipped inside, my body aching from the long day. All I wanted was a mug of hot chocolate and then my bed. When I left seven hours earlier, I'd thought my biggest concern was making sure I didn't drink too much so that I didn't have a hangover the next day. Now, all I could think about was finding Kiera, bringing her home, and making sure her ex could never harm her again.

"Hey," a deep male voice said from the darkness.

"Son of a bitch! Who's there?" I cried, automatically reaching into my bag for the dagger. I pulled it out, clutching the hilt, and was surprised to see a flash of magic crackle over the blade.

A light quickly flickered to life and Jax Williams, the man I'd been half in love with my entire life, was standing there wide-eyed, staring at the magic-infused dagger in my hand. "Uh, Marion?" he asked, nodding toward the dagger. "What's that?"

"Sorry." I slipped the dagger back into my bag and dropped

the bag on an end table near the couch. "You scared the shit out of me. How did you get in? I didn't even see your truck out front."

"My truck is in the shop, so I rode my motorcycle. It's out front. And Ty let me in." He was frowning at me. "Was that okay? I sent a text letting you know I'd be here."

He had? I quickly grabbed my phone out of my back pocket and found the unopened message right there. "Damned phone. It looks like I just didn't hear the alert. I'm sorry. It's been a hell of a night, and I just wasn't expecting anyone to be here."

He raised one eyebrow. "Not even Tandy? Because she's in the guestroom."

I quickly glanced over at the hallway that led to Ty's old room. Ty was my adopted son in every way except in the eyes of the law. He and his boyfriend had just moved to the apartment above the garage a few days ago, but they still came in the house to eat some meals with me and raid the refrigerator. "Honestly, I forgot that Tandy had come up for a few days. Like I said, it's been one hell of a night."

"Was the party that bad? Tandy was a little tipsy when she stumbled in, so I didn't get a full rundown. Or even any coherent information at all." He opened his arms, inviting me into his embrace. I didn't hesitate. After the evening I'd had, all I wanted was to fall into his arms and forget about everything for a few hours.

"It was… how you'd expect it to be," I said, wrapping my arms around him and burying my face in his shoulder. "Almost-naked men gyrating about while women screamed and threw money. Lennon seemed to have a good time, and that's all that matters."

Jax held me close, and I just melted into him, grateful for his embrace. "What is it? What happened?"

I hadn't been planning on telling him about Kiera. I believed her when she said that anyone who knew about her ex was in danger. After getting to know her, I knew she wasn't one for hysterics. She lived a lowkey life and took most things in stride. But any mention of her ex, and she'd instantly tense.

The last thing I wanted to do was put Jax in danger. But how could I keep this from him? If I was going to be doing everything in my power to find her, I couldn't keep him in the dark. Not if I wanted this relationship to work. As a matchmaker, I already knew that lies or lies by omission were the quickest way to torpedo a relationship. Besides, hiding things wasn't in my nature.

"Let's sit down," I said, leading him to the couch. After we were settled, I turned to face him. "What I'm about to tell you could put you in danger. But if you want to be involved with me then I think I have to tell you so you can make your own decisions."

He narrowed his eyes at me. "What decisions? The decision to be with you or not?"

I swallowed hard and nodded. "Yes. There's… something I was a part of a few years back that puts a target on my back. I thought it was over, but it turns out it's not. If the people involved come after me, they'll come after the people close to me, too."

"You know I'm not going to just walk out that door." He reached out and threaded his fingers through mine. "Especially if you're in danger. I think you need to tell me what's on your mind, Marion."

I'd known he'd say that, but I had to give him the choice. I closed my eyes for just a moment and then told him everything. About the day I drove a stranger from that small town in Utah all the way to LA. How she'd told me just enough about her situation so that I'd understand the danger she faced but not enough to know exactly who she'd run from or just *how much* danger she was really in. And then about Hollister's visit and Joy's vision.

Jax was silent, taking in everything I'd said.

My nerves were jumping, waiting for him to say something. Anything. Would this be where he walked out? Had I stepped into something so huge that he wouldn't want anything to do with it? No one wanted to be on the radar of someone connected who could make your life a living hell.

"You're incredible. You know that?" he said almost reverently.

"Um, what?" I asked, taken aback. I hadn't been expecting that reaction.

"You helped someone you didn't even know escape a dangerous situation, took her in, and then were there for her for years when she had no one else. Most people wouldn't do that, Marion." He reached out and tenderly tucked a lock of my red hair behind one ear. "Of course you're going to help this Hollister person find her. You wouldn't be you if you didn't."

Fresh tears stung my eyes and I quickly blinked them back. "I'm sure lots of people would've done what I did."

"Doubtful. Most people, I've learned, just want to live their comfortable lives and not deal with anything that could disrupt their safe bubbles. That's not necessarily wrong; it just means that most people wouldn't put a stranger first."

"I couldn't just leave her there. I wouldn't have been able to live with myself."

"I know. And that's one of the reasons you're special. One of the many reasons why I want to be with you whether our auras are compatible or not. I just don't care about that. I care about you and the person that's inside here." He touched his fingers to my chest just over my heart. "You're a good person, Marion, and I'll do whatever it takes to help you find your friend."

"Oh, no. You don't have to do that," I said automatically.

He raised both his eyebrows and jerked back a little. "You don't think I'm going to just sit back while you put yourself in the line of fire, do you? Because I'm telling you right now, that's not going to happen."

"No, I..." I shook my head. "I just don't want *you* in the line of fire."

"I'm a firefighter, Marion. I think I can manage," he said with a soft smile.

I let out a little chuckle. "Yeah, okay. But if anything happens to you..." Shaking my head, I reached for him, placed both my hands on his cheeks, and leaned in to kiss him. This man was everything to me. The thought of losing him made my chest ache.

"Right back atcha, Marion," he said softly before pulling me closer and deepening the kiss.

I was breathless when he finally pulled back.

Jax grinned at me. "There's food in the kitchen. Do you want to eat something?"

"There's food?" My voice was a little husky, filled with the need he'd stirred in me.

"Manicotti," he said. "But if you're hungry for something else..." He pumped his eyebrows, making it clear exactly what he thought I was hungry for.

Chuckling, I stood and held my hand out to him. As we walked into the kitchen, I said, "You realize that manicotti is the last thing I should be eating, right?"

"A little cheese and pasta won't kill you."

That's what he thought. I could already feel my fat cells

adhering to my thighs with just the thought of wolfing down the cheesy goodness at well past midnight. That wasn't going to stop me though. I loved manicotti, and Jax knew it.

"Tell me there's wine to go with it," I said as I took a seat at my table that was already set with two place settings.

Jax produced a bottle of red and filled a wine glass for me. "It's not Italian without wine."

I smiled up at him. "You're the best. You know that, right?"

He gave me a mischievous grin. "I'll show you my best after dinner."

That heat was back, coiling in my lower belly. "Promise?"

Jax sat next to me, slipped his hand over the back of my neck and then leaned in, brushing his lips lightly over mine. "Promise," he whispered.

A shiver of anticipation skated over my skin, and suddenly I had no interest in the manicotti. All I wanted was to get lost in Jax. Let him help drown out all the worry and fear that had been fueling me ever since Hollister had shown up at the club.

But before I could demand he take me to the bedroom and strip away all my clothes, he sat back in his chair and turned his attention to the dinner sitting in front of us. "I've been waiting for this ever since your aunt Lucy dropped it off this morning."

"Lucy made this?" I asked, a smile tugging at my lips as I thought of my aunt.

"Yep. She said she made one for your dad and that it was just as easy to make a second one for her favorite niece."

All thoughts of skipping dinner to hightail it into the bedroom fled. There was no turning away from Aunt Lucy's manicotti. The woman was a genius when it came to Italian cooking.

We were halfway through our dinner when Jax said, "I'm coming with you tomorrow when you search for Kiera's car."

"No. That's not a good idea," I said automatically.

"Why?" he asked, eyeing me.

"Because, Jax," I said, sounding exasperated. "Like I already said before, I don't want you to become a target."

"Then it's not a good idea for you to go either. Call that Hollister guy and tell him he's on his own," he said with a shrug, making it sound like the discussion was over.

"Jax! You know I'm not going to do that." I pressed my fingers to my temple, trying to stave off a headache.

"Then I guess it looks like we're both going." He gave me a forced smile and then shoveled in another bite of manicotti.

"Son of a... Dammit, Jax. You're not going to budge on this, are you?"

He shook his head. "Nope."

"Fine. We're supposed to meet at the Bird's Eye Café at seven."

"I'll be ready when you are." He placed his hand over mine and squeezed. "See? That wasn't so hard, was it?"

I grumbled at him. And even though I desperately wanted him to stay out of this situation so that he'd be safe, deep inside, I was glad he'd be by my side.

CHAPTER 5

"*R*eady?" I asked Jax. Fatigue weighed me down, and if it hadn't been for the infusion of coffee, I'd still be stumbling around in the dark. I didn't do well on less than five hours of sleep.

"Yeah." He pressed his hand to the small of my back and guided me out the front door.

The sky was inky purple, indicating the sun was just starting to rise, and sea salt filled the slight breeze. It was just the type of morning that was perfect for taking a walk on the beach. The thought made me think of Kiera and her last few hours before she was abducted. What had she been doing at that beach? Who had she been waiting for? And why had she been headed north toward Premonition Pointe?

None of it made sense. Hadn't she told Garrison she was headed out to get her wedding dress? Why, then, had she ended up spending the day driving up the coast? Surely she'd have used a local shop for her dress. She must have. Garrison would've known if she was headed that far out of town. None of it made any sense. If she'd been headed to see me, surely she'd have given me a heads up.

"Just go then!" someone shouted right before a door slammed.

I turned to see Ty standing on the top step of the stairs that led to the garage apartment. He was holding a duffel bag and a dog carrier as he stared at the front door. "Kennedy," he called. "Come on. It's just an interview."

There was no response.

"What's that about?" Jax asked me.

I shook my head. "I have no idea." I hit the Unlock button on my key fob. The car made a short honking sound as the lights flashed.

Ty turned to look at us and hung his head as he quickly made his way down the stairs. He came to a stop beside me.

"Everything okay?" I asked him.

He shook his head. "Apparently not. Kennedy's mad because I have an interview for a project in LA this afternoon."

A pang of sadness hit me right in the chest. "You're considering moving back?"

He shook his head. "No. It's a temporary sound job. Just four weeks, but it's working for a major film company. I can't turn it down if they're offering."

Ty had gone to school for sound mixing and had worked on a number of independent projects. But he was able to move to Premonition Pointe because he did a lot of work for games and was able to do that from home. But his real ambition was to work on movies.

A weight lifted off my chest. The truth was I really loved having him around and was glad he lived above my garage. I'd never be anything but supportive of the life he wanted to lead, but if he stayed close, I wouldn't complain. I smiled at him.

"That sounds promising. Why is Kennedy upset?" I gestured to the dog carrier where his Yorkie had her head pressed against the mesh opening. "And why are you taking Paris Francine with you if it's just an interview?"

"Kennedy's upset because he says he doesn't want to go back to LA and that if I go, he'll have to find somewhere else to live. I tried to tell him he can just stay here, but he says he can't take advantage of you like that. He told me if I get the job to just stay and to take Paris with me because he won't have the ability to take care of her when he moves out."

I frowned as I glanced at the light shining in the garage apartment. "No one is taking advantage of me."

Ty shook his head. "That's not how he sees it. No matter what I say, he seems to think he can't stay here unless I'm here."

"I'll talk to him," I said, placing a hand on Ty's arm and squeezing lightly. "Go to your interview and knock them dead. I'm sure Tandy won't mind if you stay in her guest house again if you get the job. And she loves dogs, so Paris isn't going to be a problem."

He grinned. "She already offered last night. But she was drunk, so..."

I laughed. "You know she meant it. Go. Get on the road. Call me when you get there so I know you made it safely."

"Will do." He sighed as he glanced back at the garage apartment once more, but then he leaned in and kissed me on the cheek. "Thanks, Mama Marion. I don't know what I'd do without you."

"Right back at you, kid." I gave him a quick hug and watched as he stowed Paris in the back seat and then hopped into his car and drove away.

Ten minutes later, Jax and I walked into Bird's Eye Café and got in line. I spotted Hollister immediately. The man was sitting near the window with a paper cup in his hand, glaring at me. "He's here," I said, gesturing toward him.

"Go on. I'll get your coffee and muffin," Jax said.

I gave him a quick kiss and headed over to Hollister.

"Who's that?" he asked, staring at Jax.

"Jax Williams. He's going with us today." I sat across from Hollister, ignoring that tingle at the base of my spine. I wasn't sure why that spark was always there when I was in Hollister's presence. The man's eyes were ringed with dark circles, and he was due for a shave.

"Looks like someone didn't take Kiera's warning seriously after all," he said, glaring at Jax. "Is that man your boyfriend?"

"Yes." There was no need for any other explanation.

"I'm driving." Hollister stood and started moving toward the door.

"You're not even going to wait for us to get our coffee?" I asked, following after him and gesturing to Jax that we'd be outside.

"If you'd been on time, we wouldn't be having this conversation." He unlocked his BMW and slid into the driver's seat.

Jax came striding out of the café with a paper bag and two coffee cups. His shoulders were tense and he had a scowl on his face.

"Something's wrong," I said, studying his face. "What happened?"

"I just got a call. There's been an accident at one of my construction sites. I have to go." He handed me the paper bag and one of the coffees. "I really don't want to, but I don't have a choice."

"I understand," I said, relief and regret warring with each

other in my gut. "Go. Take my car." I handed him the keys to my SUV. "Captain Crankypants is insisting on driving anyway. I'll have him drop me off at home."

Jax took the keys, gave me a quick kiss, told me to be careful, and then took off.

I slid into the passenger seat, and before I even had my seatbelt buckled, Hollister peeled out of the parking lot. I scowled at him. "It won't do anyone any good to get us killed."

"Yeah, Captain Crankypants," Celia said, popping into the back seat. "If you kill my boss, I'll haunt you so hard you won't even be able to take a piss without an audience."

"Celia? What are you doing here?" I asked the ghost.

"Keeping an eye on you. What do you think I'm doing?" she asked incredulously. "Someone needs to make sure you don't get thrown over a bluff into the sea."

"Thanks, I guess," I said dryly.

Hollister glared at Celia and then at me. "Captain Crankypants?"

"If the moniker fits..." Celia said and sat back against the soft leather.

"Does this ghost belong to you?" Hollister asked.

"Sort of. She works for me," I said, trying to relax into the seat even as he sped up and took a corner as if he were racing the Indy 500.

"Why am I not surprised?"

I wasn't sure what he meant by that, but I decided not to ask. "Did you get something from Garrison that the coven can use to try a finding spell?"

"In the glove compartment," he said.

"He's a real conversationalist, isn't he?" Celia said, her head poking out between the two front seats.

"What are you expecting me to say?" Hollister asked. "Do

you want me to wax poetic about the locket Garrison bought her for their first anniversary? Or the fact that she never takes it off, but that as soon as she headed out of town without telling anyone, she left it on her dresser? That Garrison is now questioning if she's left him because of it?"

"Yes," Celia and I said at the same time.

"All of that is important," I elaborated. "Why did she take it off if she usually doesn't?"

"How the hell should I know?" Hollister asked.

"I wasn't expecting you to know the answer," I muttered as I jotted that information down in my phone. It was one more clue. I didn't know how it tied in with her actions, but even I had to admit that it didn't look good. What if she had been having second thoughts and had left Garrison? What if she was too afraid that she'd put him in danger by marrying him? She might have gotten cold feet. Maybe she knew her ex was closing in on her and that's why she left. I pressed a hand to my stomach, trying to stop the dread from churning. That theory was more than plausible.

We rode down the coast as Celia peppered Hollister with questions, most of which he ignored.

"You must make some decent coin to afford a car like this," she said to him.

He grunted but didn't confirm or deny her observation.

"I bet the babes just fall at your feet. You're a little scruffy right now, but that five o'clock shadow you had last night…" She pressed her fingertips to her lips and kissed them. "Perfection. What I wouldn't do to feel that cheek on my inner thigh."

Hollister coughed as he eyed her in the rearview mirror.

"Celia," I said in a warning tone. "Don't you already have someone to torture like this? What happened to Danny?"

"Oh, he's around. He just doesn't have as much energy as I do, so I have to get my kicks somewhere while he's recharging."

"And it had to be here?" Hollister asked.

I chuckled because it was exactly what I'd been thinking.

Celia huffed at both of us. "You're going to regret sassing me when it turns out that I solve this for you."

"Probably," I said, knowing just how useful the ghost could be.

Hollister gave me a skeptical look.

"Hey, it's handy to have someone who can pop in and out and eavesdrop on people. If we get any line on who abducted Kiera, we can send in Celia. She's kind of like a secret weapon."

"More like a highly irritating one," Hollister said and started to slow at a turnout.

"You'll regret you said that," Celia said and disappeared into thin air.

I chuckled. "That's one way to get rid of her. You're lucky. I've never had that kind of success."

"You're a saint to put up with that all the time," he said once we were out of the vehicle.

"Not really. She grows on a person."

"Doubtful." Hollister glanced around and then walked over to the edge.

I followed and quickly saw that there wasn't an easy way to get down to the beach. "This isn't the place where Kiera stopped."

Hollister agreed with my assessment. After four more turnout stops, we finally found one that looked like it was plausible as Kiera's stopping point.

"There's no food truck," I said, squinting as I took in the parking area.

"That doesn't mean there wasn't one here three days ago," he said.

"True." We walked around the area, looking for... I don't know what we were looking for. Anything that might give us a clue that Kiera had been there. After scouring the parking lot and then walking down the beach, we made our way back up to Hollister's car. I was about to slip back into the passenger seat when an RV that had been parked at the north end of the lot eased its way back onto the highway.

"Wait," I said and walked over to the garbage cans that had been hiding behind the RV.

Hollister followed me, grumbling about not wanting to waste time.

I held my hand up, indicating he needed to wait a moment. And then I pointed at the debris on the ground. "Look!"

Hollister crouched down and picked up a paper cup that had a stylized J on it.

"It came from that food truck. It was either here or someone threw that cup away the next time they stopped," I said. Before waiting for an answer, I pulled the lid off the garbage can and peered inside. "Paydirt."

"You're not kidding." Hollister used a stick to sift through the pile of food wrappers and paper cups. There was no doubt the food truck had been there recently.

"Too bad the truck isn't here today," I said.

"We can keep looking for it," Hollister offered.

I nodded. We spent the next two hours searching up and down the coast for that food truck, only to come up empty. There weren't even any leftover food wrappers in any of the other garbage receptacles.

We made our way back to the turnout where we'd found

the food truck's garbage. "I think it's clear this is where she stopped," I said.

"I agree, but I'm not sure how this helps us. She's not here, and there's no one to ask if they saw her," Hollister said.

"It means we can start looking for the section of road where Kiera went missing. See if there are any clues there." I pointed to the road. "Head north. I'll keep my eyes peeled."

"We've been up and down this road a couple of times now. If her car was parked along the side, don't you think we would've found it by now?"

"Maybe, but what else are we going to do? Give up?" I yelled at him, beyond frustrated. A flash of light that looked like it originated at my feet illuminated the car.

"What the fuck was that?" Hollister put the car in park and stared down at my feet.

I stared, too, my eyes going wide. The light had come from my bag. More specifically, it had come from the dagger I'd left in my bag. Hey, if I was going to run around looking for someone who'd been abducted, a weapon was only a smart choice, right? I reached down and picked up the bag, the blue blade shining brightly in the dim lighting of the car.

"Holy shit." Hollister jumped out and came around to my side. After yanking the door open, he pulled me out along with my bag. "That dagger is telling you something."

I peered into my bag. "What do you mean, telling me something? It's just glowing blue. It's been doing that since last night."

"But only when you were touching it, right?" he asked.

I thought back and then nodded. "Yeah, I guess so. What difference does it make?"

"The difference is that the dagger gets its energy from the one touching it. If you're not touching it, the energy is coming from something else. Something magical in the air. It's telling you that someone has used a spell here recently."

I sucked in a sharp breath. "You think whoever took Kiera is a witch?"

"Could be. Or maybe it's just a coincidence, but I'm not one for brushing things off. If it looks like a duck and walks like a duck… You get it."

I did. I wasn't one for brushing things off as coincidence either. Especially when it came to magic. "Okay. We could try a spell to ask the magic to reveal itself."

"You can do that?" he asked looking intrigued.

"No. Or at least I don't think so. I've never tried before. My power has always been pretty concentrated on aura reading," I answered honestly. "But something tells me you can."

He shook his head. "Sadly, no. That's not one of the tricks I have up my sleeve." He eyed the dagger still lying in my bag and added, "Your power is no longer rooted just in reading auras." He nodded at the dagger. "Take that and ask it to show you any recent spells."

I was convinced that this was going to be a waste of time, but since I wanted to get on the road to see if we could find Kiera's car and any more clues, I decided to humor him. What was the worst that would happen? Nothing?

Ha. If only. How naive I was.

CHAPTER 6

*W*ith the waves crashing down along the surf, I stood facing away from the ocean, holding the dagger out in front of me. The sun glinted off the glowing blue tip, creating a gorgeous ray of light that fell along the grassy bluff. The parking lot was to the left and a rocky cliff to the right with the road in front of me. I'd walked the area, stopping only when that tingle at the base of my spine was most pronounced.

I didn't know why, but that tingle had become a magical beacon of some sort, and although my aura-reading abilities had been all but decimated, I was starting to wonder if I should thank Pixie, the woman who'd cursed me. While her curse made my job as a matchmaker harder, it seemed to have given me the gift of intuition, which wasn't anything to balk at.

Keeping my voice steady exactly as I'd witnessed the coven do each time they worked their magic around the coven circle, I called, "Goddess of the ocean, hear my call. With the power bestowed to me and this dagger, show me the spells cast upon this land."

The dagger sparked with magic, the current crackling over the blade and then the hilt until power seemed to stream right into my fingertips. The magic was like a bolt of lightning right to my spine, sending my back arching and my arms up in the air as the dagger hovered above me.

"Holy hell," I heard someone say.

I thought it must be Hollister, but I couldn't see him. I couldn't see *anything*. My vision had turned pure white before plunging me into complete darkness.

Someone cried out. Was it me? I wasn't sure.

Static filled my ears, and I started to wonder if this was what it was like when someone died. I'd lost touch with reality. I couldn't feel my limbs. My world was complete chaos.

Faces flickered through my mind. Ty. Lucy. My dad. Tandy. And Jax.

"Jax," I whispered.

"I'm here, Marion," someone said, but I knew for certain it wasn't my Jax. Not the man I'd spent a lifetime waiting for. "I've got you," he said.

I turned my head frantically, looking for the source of the voice, but was never able to find it. The faint scent of lavender filled my senses and then intensified to the point my stomach rolled with nausea.

"Goddess of the ocean!" the voice called. "Release Marion from this hold. Bring her back to her loved ones. Release the spell!"

All darkness suddenly vanished, and if it hadn't been for the strong arms that caught me, I'd have crumbled to the ground, my limbs too weak to hold me up.

"Marion?" the voice asked frantically. "Are you all right? Look at me."

I blinked up into the worried expression of a man I

recognized but couldn't place. The lavender scent had faded, but wasn't completely gone.

"Hey," he said gently and pushed a lock of hair out of my eyes. "You're okay now. I promise."

"Who...?" I started to ask but then shook my head. I knew who he was; I just couldn't recall his name. What the hell was his name?

"It's okay. You're okay," the man said soothingly. "The spell just zapped your short-term memory. It'll come back any moment now. That's what happens when a chaos spell is triggered."

"Chaos spell?" I croaked out.

The man carried me across a section of pavement, and when he got to a black car, he set me gently on my feet. My knees instantly buckled.

"Oomph," I said as I clutched at his button-down shirt. "My legs are jelly."

"I can see that." He yanked the car door open and then carefully tucked me inside. Once he had the seatbelt locked in place, he produced a bottle of water and said, "Drink this."

I did as I was told, gulping down half the bottle before I came up for air. My head started to clear, but my heart was still racing. At least my nausea had disappeared, along with the cloying lavender scent. I quickly glanced around for the dagger and found it lying on the floorboard, the blue tinge of light gone. "What happened?"

Hollister put the car into gear and pulled out onto the highway, heading north.

"You called up a spell that had been cast in that parking lot. It was really strong, so I'm guessing it happened very recently. Like in the last two or three days."

"That was a spell? What exactly was it supposed to do?" I

asked, taking another sip of water. With each swallow, the dull ache in my skull lessened.

"It was a chaos spell meant to make people forget what they saw in the general vicinity."

"Like someone being abducted?" I frowned at Hollister. "But that didn't happen there."

"Right. That's our assumption. But it could make people forget they saw Kiera or the people who were following her." Hollister eased into a corner, going slower than he had before.

I scanned the sides of the road, looking for any signs of a blue Honda. "We don't know that Kiera's abductors cast that spell. It could have been anyone."

"True. But it was really strong." His voice turned cold as he added, "It could have killed you if I hadn't gotten it to release you."

"What? You're not serious, are you?" I asked, turning quickly to stare at him. My head swam as the nausea came roaring back. I pressed one hand to my stomach and the other to my forehead. "Ouch. Son of a bitch. That was a bad idea."

"I am serious." Hollister slowed and pulled off to the side of the road. "That spell was nasty. It took a powerful witch to cast it."

That was not what I wanted to hear. I glanced around at the side of the road. "Why are we stopping here?"

He pointed at the dagger. It was once again glowing blue. "That's why."

"Oh, no. I'm not asking it to reveal any more spells. You said the last one could've killed me, and considering I feel like I've been run over by a bus, I'm inclined to believe you. So don't even ask."

"I wasn't going to." He climbed out of the car and hurried to my side, holding the door open for me.

I stared at his outstretched hand. "What are you going to do? Put our noses to the ground and sniff out any magic?"

He chuckled softly. "No, but you can if you feel strongly about it. I figured we'd search the area and see if there are any clues. There are a couple of tire tracks in the dirt. This could be the abduction point."

"Yeah, okay." I glanced at the dagger, considered leaving it in the car, and then changed my mind. At this rate, I was going to need it one way or another. Fatigued and with a slight headache, I followed Hollister to the edge of the road.

"See here? This is where the first car pulled over. It looks messy and like they were going too fast. This isn't a planned stop," Hollister said, pointing at the jagged shape of the tracks. "There's another set that is just as reckless that ends up just behind the first."

"I see it. But again, this could be anyone. How do we know it was Kiera?" I stared down at the dagger, hoping it had some sort of clue. But the only thing it did was crackle with magic. The feeling made me uneasy. The last time it had done that, I'd needed someone to save me from a powerful spell.

"We don't. At least not yet," he said and started to inspect the area, careful not to disturb the tracks.

"What are we looking for?" I asked, peering at the dirt beneath our feet.

"Anything that could've belonged to Kiera. If you find something, it might be a clue that could tell us if we're on the right track."

I sucked up my skepticism and joined him in his search. I was just about to give up when something glinted at me from the dirt near the mile marker. "Hollister, what's this?" I bent and brushed the dirt away from the shining silver.

He kneeled next to me and then sucked in a sharp breath.

After pulling out a handkerchief, he gingerly picked it up, careful not to disturb any prints.

"It's a dagger… just like mine," I said, recognizing the design on the hilt. "Only it's smaller."

"It was designed to fit Kiera's grip," he said quietly before walking over to his car and rummaging around until he found a plastic bag. After stowing the dagger away, he jumped back into the car. "Get in. We need to find someone who can run prints on that dagger."

"How do you know it's Kiera's?" I asked, certain I probably already knew the answer.

"I made it for her."

Without saying a word, I pulled out my phone and made a call. "Gigi, I need a favor."

"You got it," my witchy friend answered without hesitation.

"Can Sebastian get some fingerprints run on something? We need it to be discrete. No one in law enforcement can find out about it."

"You found something." It was a statement, not a question.

"We did. Is it possible?"

"Yes. Come to the house. I'll have Sebastian make a call."

"Thanks, Gigi." I pressed End and slipped my phone back into my pocket.

"Who's Sebastian?" Hollister asked, pressing his foot into the gas.

"He's an attorney."

"You trust him?"

"I wouldn't ask him for this if I didn't," I said and then turned to stare out the window, praying this was the break we needed.

CHAPTER 7

J walked into my house, wrung out from the day's events. After dropping the small dagger off at Gigi's for Sebastian, I'd suggested that we research impound lots to see if we could find Kiera's car and search the internet for the food truck with the stylized J logo. Hollister had offered to take on the impound lots and insisted that I get some rest. It was obvious he was worried about me after the chaos spell incident. I'd promised to research the food truck while I took it easy and then we'd each report back when we found anything.

After a text to Jax to let him know I was home safe, I grabbed a snack from the kitchen before plopping down in front of my computer. I'd just typed *food trucks near Premonition Pointe* into my browser when the guestroom door opened and Tandy appeared. Her curly dark hair was tied up in a messy bun and held in place with a pen. She was dressed in a formfitting T-shirt and cotton pants that hit just above her ankles. It was the type of outfit that I hadn't been able to wear since high school, but she looked adorable.

"Hey," I said to my friend. "I wondered if you were going to join me."

"What else would I do?" she asked with a laugh. "Besides, I've spent enough time working on my latest script. I need someone to entertain me while I binge popcorn."

"You'll have to make it. I don't think I can move," I said, stifling a yawn. My eyes watered and my entire body felt heavy as if I were coming down with the flu.

"You don't look so hot," she said, eyeing me.

"I'm fine," I insisted. "I just didn't sleep all that well." It wasn't a complete lie. Less than five hours of shuteye didn't qualify as a good night's rest.

"There's plenty you aren't telling me," she said without judgment. "Is everything okay with you?"

"I'm fine. It's not me. It's Kiera. She's gone missing."

Tandy let out a small gasp. They'd met through me and were friendly acquaintances, but as far as I knew, Tandy didn't know anything about Kiera's past and I was going to keep it that way. It was bad enough that I'd brought Jax and the coven into this. I wouldn't be risking Tandy's wellbeing, too.

"I'm working with the coven to try to find her," I said.

"Are the authorities looking for her?"

I bit back a wince. Of course she'd ask that. "No. There's no evidence of foul play, so there isn't anything for them to investigate. But I know Kiera. She wouldn't leave Garrison like that."

Tandy spent the next few minutes grumbling about how useless law enforcement could be, and because I didn't want to have to lie to her further, I just let her as I continued the search for the elusive food truck. When my search failed miserably, I said, "Hey, have you ever seen a food truck with a stylized J on the side?"

Her brows pinched as she thought it over. "Hmm, we have a lot of food trucks at our filming locations, but I'm not sure I've ever noticed what each one is called. It's always the burrito truck, or the avocado fries truck, or the sandwich truck. That kind of thing."

"This one is sandwiches," I said, hoping that would trigger something for her.

But Tandy shook her head. "I can ask my PA. She might know."

"That would be great." I closed the computer and leaned my head back against the couch. "We don't have a lot to go on, but we know Kiera stopped at a food truck shortly before she went missing."

"I'm on it." Tandy stood and fished her phone out of her pocket. A moment later, I heard her ask Kimmie to search for all the names and logos of the food trucks that were invited on set, and when she exhausted those, to research food trucks that frequented the highway up and down the coast.

When Tandy ended the call, I gave her a grateful smile. "Thank you."

"Anything for you, babe. Now, let's get you up off this couch and into the sunshine. What do you say?"

I groaned. "You're not going to make me walk on the beach, are you? I don't think my legs can take it today."

"Nope. You're going to sit out on the porch while I make us a late lunch." Tandy led me outside, brought me a blanket to keep warm, and then disappeared back into the house.

I sat on my porch, not minding the chill as I listened to the faint crashing of waves, grateful my friend was there to make sure I took care of myself. Normally I was never at home in the middle of the day even on a Saturday. There was too much work to be done getting the dating agency up and running, but the thought of sifting through inquiries and helping people plan their dates just seemed so trivial when all I could do was think about Kiera and pray that she was safe.

Footsteps sounded on the stairs that led to the apartment over the garage. I glanced over to see Kennedy hauling a large suitcase and a duffel bag down the stairs. "Kennedy?"

He paused at the bottom of the steps as he met my eyes and muttered something to himself before he dropped his stuff and walked over. "I didn't realize you were here. Where's your car?"

"Jax has it." I eyed his luggage before turning my attention back to him. "Where are you headed?"

He glanced away, his shoulders hunched and a defiant expression on his face. "I need to move out."

"Why's that?" I asked curiously.

"Ty got that job down in LA." His tone was void of emotion.

"He did?" That was news to me. I'd gotten a text that he'd arrived safe, but hadn't heard from him otherwise. Had they offered it to him on the spot? He'd only left that morning for the interview.

"He called about a half hour ago." Kennedy stared off in the direction of the ocean as he shoved his hands into the pockets of his too-loose jeans. "They want him to start in two days."

I studied the young man. He had brilliant blue eyes, gorgeous curly hair that most women would die for, and a long, lean frame. He was striking in a Hollywood kind of way. He hadn't had the best home life, and while he could sometimes give off a tortured vibe, in the last two weeks he'd come out of his shell. When he was relaxed, he was kind and funny and a joy to be around. But today, he just seemed despondent and defeated.

"You think because Ty is going to be away for a month that you need to move out?" I asked gently.

"Yes. I can't stay here and take advantage of you."

"You're not taking advantage if I'm the one who is offering," I said.

He just shook his head. "I'm an adult. I need to find my own way."

I could appreciate a young person wanting to strike out on his own, but Kennedy had recently been cast out by his own family. The problem was I couldn't shake the feeling that he wasn't emotionally ready to be completely independent, not after what went down with his parents, but it wasn't like I could stop him. He was in his early twenties and had every right to live his life in whatever way he thought best. "Would you mind sitting down with me for a minute before you leave?"

Kennedy ran a hand through his already tousled curls and let out a sigh. I could tell that he just wanted to take his stuff and go. He hadn't been expecting to have to explain his actions when he'd decided to leave. That was obvious. Nonetheless, he nodded once and sat in the chair next to me.

"I respect the fact that you want to find your own way. I really do," I said kindly. "That's an admirable trait in anyone."

He just nodded as he continued to stare out at my quiet street.

"But I wouldn't feel right if I didn't make it clear that you are more than welcome here. I don't see you as a burden in any way. Our home is your home. If this decision to move out is right for you, then go with my blessing. However, if you think it's because you're not welcome or we don't want you here, that's just not the case. I enjoy your company. And I know Ty wants you to stay, too."

"I just can't stay here without Ty," he said, turning so I couldn't see his expression.

I wanted to ask him why but held back. I had a feeling that whatever was driving this decision had more to do with his relationship with Ty than anything else, and I didn't think it was my place to pry. "Okay," I said reluctantly as that tingle of magic flared to life at the base of my spine. "Just know that if you need anything, a friend, a meal, a bed, I'm here, regardless of what's going on between you and Ty. Do you understand?"

The young man turned to me, his eyes glassy with unshed tears. He reached over and squeezed my hand. "Ty is a really lucky guy. I hope he knows that. Thank you, Marion. I appreciate everything more than you know."

"You're very welcome. It's been my pleasure."

He nodded, rose from the chair, and then retrieved his stuff. I expected a car service to arrive, but instead, he heaved the duffel over his shoulder and dragged the rolling suitcase behind him as he started walking down my street, headed in the direction of town.

"Kennedy? Do you need a ride somewhere?" I called when I realized he intended to walk wherever he was headed.

"No thank you," he called back. "You've already done more than enough."

Dread pooled in the pit of my stomach, and I just knew that this was a mistake. I couldn't let him go without trying one more time. I jumped up out of my chair and hurried over to him. "What if you worked for me in exchange for room and board. You could do my yardwork, repaint the garage, take care of the upkeep, that kind of thing. That wouldn't be taking advantage of me. In fact, I'd love for someone to do all the things I never have time to do."

"Thank you, but I just can't. I appreciate all this, but we both know Jax will do all of those things."

He was right. Jax would handle the minor fixes my house needed if I asked. However, I wasn't ever going to ask my boyfriend to be my built-in yard boy and handyman. I was far more independent than that. Plus, if it meant keeping Kennedy here and away from whatever it was that had my hackles rising, then it was worth it. "Jax doesn't have time to deal with my upkeep. Seriously, you'd be doing me a favor."

He gave me a pained expression. "Please, Marion. Just let me go. I need to do this. For me."

There wasn't anything else to say after that. As much as it pained me, I nodded once, grabbed him into a fierce hug, and then let him go, dreading every moment as I watched him walk away from me and possibly Ty.

Feeling defeated, I walked back to the porch where Tandy was waiting for me with a couple of sandwiches.

"Are you okay?" she asked, sounding concerned.

"Not really. I have a bad feeling about Kennedy leaving." I took a seat next to her and shared the blanket as she passed me a sandwich and then wrapped an arm around my shoulders, pulling me in for a sideways hug.

"He'll be back," she said, sounding confident.

I didn't have the same convictions. "I hope you're right."

CHAPTER 8

*M*y phone rang an hour later and Ty's picture flashed on the screen. "Hey," I said. "How'd the interview go?" I already knew the answer but wanted to give Ty the chance to tell me himself.

"Great! They want me to start right away, and they are offering a significant retention bonus if I stay the full four weeks. If things go well, they want me for the next project, too." He let out a small chuckle. "I guess sound guys are in short supply, and the last guy they had was poached right before they started on the project."

"That's wonderful. Good for you." Pride washed over me for the man I thought of as my son. It'd been a rough four years since we'd lost his mom, but after all that pain, there had been healing and I just knew that Trish was watching over him as proud as any mom could be. Though with the promise of another project, that might be one of the reasons why Kennedy was taking it so hard. "It sounds like a great opportunity."

"It is." Some of the excitement faded from his tone. "Kennedy moved out."

"I know. I was here when he left. I'm sorry, Ty. I tried to get him to stay, but he said he had to do this for himself."

"At least he talked to you," Ty said, sounding irritated. "He only sent me a text and told me he'd call later when he was settled."

"He seemed…"

"Selfish? Irrational? Manipulative?" Ty spouted off, his anger coming through loud and clear.

"Um, no," I said carefully. "He didn't seem like he was any of those things to me. More like sad and a little lost."

Ty let out a huff. "Well, I wouldn't know. He won't take my calls."

"I think he might just need some time," I said, trying to be diplomatic.

"Time? Really? He won't even talk to me about this. What am I supposed to do? Just give up on my career because he doesn't want me to be more than ten miles from home? I get that he's going through some stuff, but I have things too. This tantrum or whatever it is just isn't okay."

"You're right," I said soothingly. "You deserve someone who is going to support you. I'm one hundred percent on your side about that. But maybe don't write him off just yet. Sometimes people just need to work things out for themselves before they have the ability to really be a good partner to someone else."

There was a long silence on the other end of the line before he spoke again. "I think more than anything, I'm just worried about him."

"I know. Me, too."

"I'm not crazy, right? I should be taking this job."

"You're not crazy," I confirmed. "You should do what's right for you. Hopefully when it's right, you and Kennedy can come back together if that's what you both still want."

"I wouldn't know what he wants, other than for me not to leave Premonition Pointe," Ty said. "It's not like I'm leaving forever. Just until this job is done."

"Or until the one after that? Or the one after that?" I asked.

"That's not fair," he snapped. "I don't know my plans after this. And in my work, almost nothing is permanent."

"Maybe that's what scares Kennedy. After all, he did have his entire support system give up on him, and the next thing he knows, you're leaving town. Maybe he's feeling abandoned."

"That's not what I did," Ty insisted.

"I know. I'm not saying you did. I just mean that he might be feeling that way. You did nothing wrong. You know that and so do I. I bet he even knows that. But sometimes…"

"I know. You just need to give people time. I just hope it doesn't take over thirty years like it did with you and Jax."

"Ouch," I said mildly.

"Sorry."

"The truth hurts sometimes," I said, keeping my tone light. "You're right. It took us far too long to come back together, but that was mostly my fault, not his. Try to learn from my mistakes and don't close the door on Kennedy."

"Yeah. Okay." A car horn sounded in the background. "Listen, Mama Marion, I better get going. My friend Guy is here to pick me up. We're going out for drinks. Talk to you tomorrow?"

"Of course. Be safe."

"Always."

The line went dead, and I stuffed my phone in my pocket, wondering if Ty had told Kennedy about his plans to see his friends. If so, it didn't take a genius to figure out that Kennedy was feeling left out and left behind, just as he had with his family. They had some issues to work out, but it wasn't going to be tonight. And as much as I wanted to fix it for both of them, it wasn't something that I could wave a magic wand at and make everything better.

Frustrated, I walked into my kitchen and started cleaning up. Tandy had gone to take a hot shower, and I was spinning my wheels, not sure what to do. It turned out Grace hadn't been sick from too much alcohol. Instead, she was suffering from a bout of food poisoning and still wasn't up to par. It had been decided that if Grace was feeling better, Hollister and I would meet the coven the following night at sunset to try the finding spell. Gigi seemed to think that the shift in days would actually help since the full moon was scheduled to rise. It would help harness their power.

There was a knock on my door right before someone opened it and called, "Marion!"

Tazia. She was my friend who lived a few streets over.

"Come in," I called, not moving from my spot in the kitchen. Once the dishes were done, I was contemplating making a batch of peanut butter cookies. I needed something to keep my hands busy while my mind raced with thoughts of Kennedy and Kiera.

"Oh, thank the gods," Tazia said as she hurried inside. Her peasant skirt flared out behind her, and her off the shoulder blouse showed off her tanned shoulders. She always looked like she'd just stepped out of a 1970s music festival. Especially when she was bringing me sunflowers. Which was often. But this time, she'd come empty-handed. I couldn't remember the last time she'd come over without some kind of bouquet from her greenhouse.

"What's wrong?" I asked, wondering what in the fresh hell had happened now.

"I don't know exactly," she said, pressing her hand to her

forehead. "I just keep getting this weird feeling that I need to warn you that someone in your life has bad intentions."

I blinked at her. "What does that mean, exactly?"

She shook her head. "That's just it. I have no idea. But the dread started coming on earlier today, and it just keeps getting worse. So I figured I'd let you know so you can be on guard."

I dried my hands on a towel and poured a cup of coffee just to give myself a moment to process what she'd said. Someone in my life had bad intentions. "Are these bad intentions toward me or someone else?" I asked as I handed her the mug.

She took it and sat at the table. "Not sure."

Well, that was helpful, wasn't it? I made myself my own mug of coffee and sat next to her. "Explain it to me. Bad intentions could mean anything. Does it mean Ty or my dad lying to me about something they just don't want to explain? Or is it more like Jax is dating someone else and not telling me?"

"Oh, no. Nothing like that." She waved her arms in front of her rapidly as if to wave away the bad juju. "This is more like someone in your life is dangerous, and you should be wary."

Oddly enough, that explanation helped me to relax a tiny bit. This was just an extension of being involved with trying to find Kiera. Her ex wasn't exactly in my life, but he certainly was dangerous. And the longer we looked for Kiera, the higher the likelihood that I'd come in contact with him. "All right," I said, sitting back in my chair. "I'll keep that under advisement."

Tazia narrowed her eyes at me, looking a little frustrated. "You don't seem to be taking this seriously. I know I sometimes come off as being a little vague and flighty, but when I get these feelings, they almost always end up being true."

I placed my hand over hers and squeezed. "I am taking you

seriously. I didn't mean to make you think otherwise, and I really do appreciate the warning. It's just that I think I already know who the problem is. And believe me, I'm already well aware of how dangerous he can be."

Her frustration turned to concern. "You're being careful, right? Does your dad know? Oh, gosh. He's going to be so worried. Maybe he should move back in here."

"Whoa," I said. "Slow down a minute. I haven't talked to my dad yet. I'm not even sure what he's up to. You probably know more about that than I do."

Her face flushed pink as she glanced away. Clearing her throat, she said, "I am supposed to see him a little later today, but it's not like I talk to him all the time. We're just... still getting to know each other." Her forehead wrinkled as she frowned. "I think he had a breakfast date with a woman at the Bird's Eye Café this morning. So don't start thinking we're an item."

"He did?" I asked, ready to call my dad and give him a piece of my mind. If he messed things up between him and Tazia, I was really going to let him have it. The man had been dating the wrong women for years, always staying clear of the ones who might end up wanting a commitment. But I'd thought that after the last fiasco when a woman went psycho online, he'd decided to maybe try someone a little more stable. Someone like Tazia.

"I don't know for sure," she said, staring at her hands. "But I saw him having coffee with a blonde when I popped in there on my way to get my bi-weekly massage. When I stopped by his table to say hi, he looked uncomfortable, so I just left."

I let out a groan and tilted my head back to stare at the ceiling. "Dad, what are you doing?"

"Now, Marion. Don't go giving him a hard time," she

insisted. "We're not exclusive, nor have we even had that talk. We're just…"

"Getting to know each other. I know. I just don't understand him sometimes."

"I do," she said quietly. "Unfortunately, I understand all too well why he shies away from commitment. When you've been hurt like that, it's hard to open your heart to another." It was her turn to pat my hand.

For the first time since I'd met Tazia, I saw a bone-deep sadness shine through her usually sunny disposition. It made my heart ache for her. Tazia was a special woman, and I couldn't imagine why anyone would intentionally hurt her. "You've had someone walk out on you just like he did, haven't you?"

She just gave me a sad smile, stood, and patted me on the shoulder as she said, "You don't get to be my age without a few chinks in the armor. Be careful, okay, Marion? I'm not going to be able to stop worrying about you until this feeling goes away."

"I will be. I promise."

She nodded once and then walked out of my house.

I sat at the table for a long time, thinking about my dad and Tazia. I'd known instantly that they were perfect for each other, but I'd just seen firsthand how right I'd been. I only hoped that Dad wouldn't let his fears get in the way of something so special.

CHAPTER 9

*J*t was late when Jax walked in my front door. Caked with dirt and with dark circles under his eyes, he walked over and kissed me on the cheek. "I was going to head home to shower first, but I didn't have the energy. Mind if I use yours?"

"Of course not." I glanced over at Tandy, who was sitting in my oversized chair and scribbling in a notebook. "We watched a movie and had takeout. There's some leftover enchiladas in the fridge if you're hungry."

He glanced longingly at the kitchen but then shook his head. "Shower first."

When he disappeared into my room, Tandy let out a low whistle. "Damn, girl. Your restraint is off the charts. If my man had come home looking so effing hot, all dirtied up like that, there's no way my ass wouldn't be in the shower with him."

"Tandy!" I shook my head at her. But then as I heard the water filter through the pipes, I imagined Jax peeling himself out of his clothes and stepping into the spray. Someone needed to help him scrub the dirt from his back, right? My feet started to move on their own, and I heard my friend snicker behind me.

"Get it, girl," she said.

"That's what I'm always telling her," the familiar voice of Celia called out.

I quickly glanced back to see the ghost curled up on the couch. The waifish blonde was smiling, and her Kewpie-doll eyes sparkled at me. She waggled her fingers in my direction and then leaned over to look at Tandy's notebook.

"Oh, is this a new TV show idea?" Celia gushed. "Tell me you wrote in a ghost! I'd be perfect for it. No need for special effects. And full nudity isn't a problem."

Tandy eyed her as if she were considering the idea.

"Keep her in mind, Tandy," I said. "Turns out Celia's really useful to have around."

Celia beamed at me. "Thanks, Marion. You don't know how much that means to me."

I thought I did, but I just nodded and slipped into my room, shutting the door behind me. The bathroom door had been left open, and it was clear by the pile of clothes on the floor that Jax had already made it into the shower. I quickly stripped off my clothes and joined him.

"Hey," he said, his eyes heating with desire the moment he scanned my naked flesh.

"I hope you don't mind me crashing your shower."

His hands landed lightly on my hips, and instead of answering me, he pulled me close until my body was pressed against his, and then his hungry mouth devoured mine. We'd gone from zero to sixty in one second flat. My entire body started to tingle with anticipation.

This. This right here was what I'd been missing for the past three decades. Everything about Jax turned me on. His quiet steadiness. His gentle nature. The secret smile he always seemed to save for me. But most of all, it was the fire that raged between us. All it took was one touch, and my body came alive for him.

With the water sluicing over us, Jax turned me so that I was pressed against the cool tiles of the shower. He let out a low growl as he moved his lips to my neck and gently bit down on the flesh just below my ear.

Pure unadulterated need shot straight to my core, and I wrapped one leg around his hip, inviting his hard shaft to find my center.

"Gods, Marion," he whispered. "How is it possible that I never get enough of you?"

"Why question it?" I asked breathlessly, my nails digging into his back. "Just enjoy it. Enjoy me."

"I plan to." His hand held my leg in place even as he dipped his head to catch one nipple between his lips, teasing it.

I closed my eyes, reveling in the sensations he was bestowing on me. In the three-plus decades of my sexual history, no one had ever done it for me like Jax did. We were combustible.

"I need you, Marion," Jax growled as he shifted his hips, moving until the tip of him pressed against my center.

"Yes." My voice was hoarse, almost desperate. "Take me," I ordered.

He didn't hesitate as he thrust forward until he was completely buried inside of me.

I let out a gasp of pleasure, clutching his ass, holding him there for just a moment.

"Holy shit," he muttered. "You feel so fucking good, babe."

"You too," I said and shifted my hips just a bit, urging him to move.

He didn't need any other encouragement. With his hands flush against the tile, he pumped his hips, pounding into me over and over and over again. And when he dipped his head to scrape his teeth over the nape of my neck, I was lost in a sea of sensation.

Then he lost all control, using his hands to grip my ass and lift me completely off my feet, shifting the angle so that his shaft hit just the right spot. With both legs wrapped around his waist, my hands in his hair, and his mouth now sucking on one nipple, my body suddenly stiffened as my orgasm rolled through me, the feeling so intense that I stopped breathing.

"Fuck, fuck, fuck," he gasped out and continued to thrust into me as I rode out the pleasure. Then he buried himself in me once more as his orgasm took over. He held still, his body trembling, his breathing uneven.

I ran my hands gently down his back and let out a small chuckle. "That's one way to start the evening."

Jax buried his head in my shoulder and shook with silent laughter. "I hope we weren't too loud. That might be more than Tandy bargained for."

"Ha!" I snorted. "She's the one who suggested I should come help you scrub away that dirt."

Jax finally pulled out and set me gently on my feet. "Is that right? Looks like I owe her one then." He bent down and kissed me softly on the lips.

And when he turned me so that I was in front of him with the warm water taking away the sudden chill, I closed my eyes and leaned back into him. He ran his hands over my stomach and up to cup my breasts, all the while murmuring that I was beautiful.

Lies, I thought, trying to forget the thirty extra pounds I needed to lose and the cellulite on the backs of my thighs that would never go away. But I kept all that to myself. I knew from experience that Jax didn't like it when I pointed out my perceived flaws. So instead, I just enjoyed the attention until it was my turn to explore him.

"I came into the shower to scrub that dirt off you. I think we better get to it before the hot water runs out," I said, turning to face him.

"If you insist," he said with a sexy half smile.

"I do." The words felt weird on my lips and conjured up a scene with a white wedding dress, tons of flowers, and a DJ playing hits from the eighties. Goddess above, what in the world was going through my mind? A wedding? I was nowhere near ready for a wedding, let alone marriage.

"What is going through that head of yours?" Jax asked, sounding more curious than anything.

"Huh?" I asked, jerking my head up to meet his eyes. "Nothing. I mean, why do you ask?"

"You looked almost amused and then horrified." He narrowed his eyes suspiciously. "Tell me you're not regretting this."

I frowned. "Regretting what?"

"This." He waved a hand between us. "Shower sex with your friend in the other room. It's one thing to get carried away; it's quite another when you have to face the person who just heard you making sex noises."

"Hell no," I said, stepping in closer to rub the soap over his too-good-to-be-true abs. "I never regret sex with you. Not when it's so good it makes my toes curl."

His lips quirked with amusement as he caught one of my hands and slid it down his body until I was gripping his shaft. His half-hard cock stiffened as he pumped his hips so that he was slowly fucking my hand. "Does that mean you're ready to go again?"

I bit my lower lip, already hungry for him again. When we were like this, there was no denying the passion between us.

"That looks like a yes," he said. And this time, he turned me so that I was facing the tile, both hands pressed against the wall as he took me.

CHAPTER 10

*J*ax sat on the other side of the bed with a plate of enchiladas in his lap.

I perched next to him, my mouth open as I stared at him in shock. He'd just told me that the construction emergency was because his latest job, an office building on the north side of town, had collapsed, and all signs led to foul play. "What do you mean your latest build was sabotaged?"

"I spent the entire day with the county officials sifting through the rubble. And they found evidence of explosives in the debris, strategically placed near key supports."

"But who would do that? And why? Did you piss off someone else who bid on the job?" I asked, unable to believe anyone would do something like that. "Was anyone hurt?" I asked belatedly, horrified by the thought.

"Thankfully, no. But here's the thing... The explosives weren't your normal run-of-the-mill incendiaries," he said carefully.

"What does that mean? Like black market stuff?"

He shook his head but then shrugged as if to say *maybe*.

"The explosives were magical, meaning they were homemade and untraceable. We had to call in the Magical Task Force. They're going to run trace tests on them and see if they can match the magical signature to find out who did this."

I sat back, stunned. "That doesn't make any sense. Why would a witch target you?"

Jax let out a sardonic laugh. "Erikson, the Magical Task Force agent, seemed to suggest it could be some sort of stalker trying to get my attention."

"What? Why?" A throbbing started at my temple, and all I wanted was to turn time back a few days before everything started to fall apart.

"He asked if I'd pissed anyone off in the recent past, and I jokingly said Lennon Love's followers after it became clear I was dating someone else." He shoved a forkful of food into his mouth and closed his eyes as he savored the Mexican dish.

"So, he's implying that your new online celebrity has gained you a stalker who's willing to go so far as to blow up a construction project just to get your attention?"

"Or teach me a lesson for disrespecting Lennon or something like that."

Nothing about that theory felt right to me. "You're telling me this Erikson guy really believes that someone just blew up your building, out of the blue, with no warning signs whatsoever?"

Jax grimaced. "I wouldn't say there haven't been any warning signs."

A dull ache flared to life in my lower back, making me grimace. I shifted carefully, trying to ease the tension as I waited for Jax to elaborate. When he didn't, I said, "I know you're not going to just leave it at that. What kind of warning signs were there, Jax?"

He placed the almost empty plate on the nightstand beside him and gestured for me to move closer.

I shook my head. "I'm fine right here, thanks."

Sighing, he rested his head against the headboard and said, "I've had some disturbing online messages about the Lennon thing."

The ache intensified, and my stomach started to churn. "You didn't say anything about those."

"You're right. I didn't. But that's because I didn't take any of them seriously. When people started sending me messages that were clearly unhinged, I just blocked them. Isn't that how people handle social media trolls?"

"Yes, but not if they are sending threatening messages," I said. "Those are the ones you keep copies of just in case the person is more than a troll."

"So I've been told," he said with a look of disgust. "So now, because I've deleted all those messages, Erickson says he doesn't have much to go on. If I'd kept them, they'd investigate. Now I'm supposed to send any threatening message straight to him. He says it's not unusual for the perpetrator to try to make contact again. It's all part of the attention-seeking cycle."

"Dammit, Jax. I'm so sorry," I said, taking his hand in both of mine. "None of this would be happening if I hadn't roped you into going to that damned mixer."

"Is that what you think?" he asked, tilting his head to study me. "I'm pretty sure that even if I hadn't agreed, I'd have still been there once the fire broke out."

That tiny detail didn't make me feel any better even though he was right. He'd have been there after the fire broke out since he was a volunteer firefighter for the town of Premonition Pointe. "I wish I could say I wouldn't have roped you into going on a date with Lennon, but we both know that'd be a lie. I would've because she wanted a date with you, and I wanted her to write about a good experience with my dating agency. I never should've done that though, for a variety of reasons."

"Because you wanted me for yourself," he said with a half grin.

I rolled my eyes, but he was only speaking the truth. "Yes, I did, and it was unethical to set you two up like that, knowing you were never going to want to date her. But also because you didn't really want to go and now look what's happened. This is all my fault. I'm so sorry, Jax. You don't deserve this."

"Hey," he said softly as he wrapped an arm around my shoulders and pulled me into a sideways hug. "It isn't your fault that someone destroyed my building. It's all on them. One hundred percent. You know that. I know you know that. If it is an online stalker, then this could have happened whether I went out on a date with Lennon or not. It's only more probable because that's when I became more public. But let's face it. That annual firefighter calendar that's coming out in a couple of weeks could have the same effect. It's not like I shied away from that."

I pulled back and stared at him, completely stunned. "You posed for the firefighter calendar?"

"I did. Wearing only my turnout pants." He winked at me and grinned, flashing me that irresistible dimple on his right cheek. "Looks like we have our first sale."

I laughed. "I'll take a half dozen."

"No need to spend that much when you have the real thing right here." He pressed a kiss to my temple. "Now, tell me about your day."

I groaned and then proceeded to do as he asked. When I got to the part about revealing the chaos spell, I downplayed the effect it had on me, but only because I didn't want him to worry.

It didn't work. Concern filled his dark eyes. "That sounds dangerous, Marion. I don't like this. Not at all."

"You think I do?" I asked defensively. "Don't you think I'd love to call the police station and report her missing? Or the Magical Task Force? If I had my way, I'd be calling your guy Erickson tonight. But Kiera was adamant that her ex had ties that ran deep across all law enforcement. I don't know who to trust other than those closest to me."

"You can't blame me for worrying about you," he said quietly as he ran his hand up and down my arm soothingly. "I know you're in a tough situation. I just wish I could be by your side tomorrow. Unfortunately, I have to deal with the fallout from today's disaster."

I pressed my head against his chest, feeling the solid throb of his heartbeat against my ear. "I know. Don't think I'm not worried about you and your stalker. What if they escalate and hurt someone the next time?" The dread in my gut was starting to make my stomach churn.

"The crew and I will be careful," he said, but the words felt empty to me. Neither of us could make any promises. We didn't know what the future had in store for us. But I also knew neither of us would back down. I wouldn't give up on Kiera, and he wouldn't let some lunatic ruin his career. The only path for each of us was to keep moving forward.

IT FELT strange to be walking into my office the next morning. I wasn't scheduled to work since it was Sunday, but with Kiera still missing I needed to focus on something else. I wanted to be out looking for her, but I had no idea where that could possibly be. Gigi had said she'd let us know as soon as Sebastian had results for the prints on the small dagger we'd found.

All I knew was that I had most of the day free before I was supposed to meet the coven, and sitting around the house waiting for answers sounded like torture.

"Good morning!" Celia sang as she floated through the office. "What adventure are we going on today?"

I glanced over at the ghost, who'd stopped at the window to peer out at the street.

"You're looking at it. Unless you have a lead," I said, powering on my computer.

"Nope. All is quiet out there in the Pointe." She glanced back at me, her lips in a pout. "I swear, the people of this town wouldn't know a juicy piece of gossip if it slapped them right on the ass. The only thing anyone is talking about is the collapse of that office building that was under construction."

My ears perked up at the mention of Jax's project. "Yeah? What are they saying?"

"Just that it must've been shoddy construction, and now everyone is speculating that corners were cut to save money and that the city officials were bribed to issued permits without inspections. All boring, small-town politics crap."

I winced. That was not what I wanted to hear. "That's Jax's project, and he certainly wasn't cutting corners."

Celia shrugged. "I'm just reporting what I heard. No one was talking about a missing woman."

That figured. If the city didn't come out and make a statement about the office building, people wouldn't hesitate to speculate whether there was any basis to their gossip or not.

"How are things with Danny?" I asked Celia just so I could focus on something less stressful.

"Good." She smiled, her face lighting with happiness. "He's the best date a girl could ask for. Imagine being taken to *Abs, Buns, and Guns* every night."

"Uh, really? He takes you there?"

"Sure. He's sort of tied to the place. Hasn't figured out how to move around in the rest of the world, so we meet up there. Who's gonna say no to that?"

"As long as you're happy, I guess."

She beamed. "I am. But it does mean I have to fill my days doing something. So here I am. What's on the agenda today, boss? Need me to keep an eye on someone?"

If only I could send her to find Kiera's ex. I briefly thought about having her follow Jax but quickly nixed that idea. No doubt, she'd drive him up the wall. "Can you just keep an eye out for Kennedy? He moved out yesterday, and I'm a little worried about him. Just make sure he's safe?"

"On it." She saluted me as if I'd just given her an order. "I really like that one. I'd be more than happy to keep him in line."

"I didn't mean—" I started, but before I could finish my sentence, she'd disappeared. At least she was mostly harmless. The worst she'd do was annoy him. Right?

There was a knock on the office door, startling me. I frowned as I went to answer it. I didn't have any appointments scheduled for that morning, and if Iris was coming in, she certainly wouldn't knock. The knock sounded again, and I called out, "Coming."

A tall, perfectly groomed man with blond hair and a smooth-shaven face smiled at me once I opened the door. "Marion Matched?"

I nodded. "You found me. What can I do for you?"

"I saw all the buzz about your new agency and figured I'd stop in and see if you have time in your schedule to find a busy businessman someone special."

"Are you the busy businessman?" I asked.

He chuckled. "I am." Holding out his hand, he said, "Brixton Belford, but my friends call me Brix."

I quickly shook his hand. The moment we touched, that tingle at the base of my spine flared to life, nearly making me arch my back from the intensity of it.

"Whoa," Brix said. "That was an intense one, wasn't it?"

"You felt that?" I asked, still staring at his hand.

"All the way to my toes." He winked, and I couldn't help but be drawn in by his charm. The man was more than just handsome. He had a warmth about him that was contagious. The anxiety from the last few days eased as I invited him in, grateful to be working with someone who would be a joy to match.

Once we were sitting at my desk, I fired up the computer and turned to him. "Now, tell me what you're looking for."

He sat back, propped one ankle on his knee, and appeared to think about his answer before he said, "Someone feisty, strong, and fun as hell to be around. Someone loyal. Spontaneous. Adventurous. But most importantly, someone who just has that spark." He glanced at my hands. "The kind you know the minute you meet someone. You know all about that... right?"

I gave him a patient smile and said, "Don't waste your best material on me. I'm sorry to say, I don't date my clients."

He laughed, his eyes glinting with mischief.

I had to admit that if I wasn't already taken, he'd be hard to resist. In addition to being classically handsome, he oozed charm.

"That's not exactly what I read on the internet, but I'll take your word for it." His tone was teasing as he leaned forward. "Honestly, Marion, I just want someone who excites me. Someone who can pick up and fly out of the country at a moment's notice but who also doesn't just want to date a rich guy. I don't like feeling used." For the first time since he'd walked through the door, there was an edge in his tone, and I had to conclude that he'd been burned before. "Can you make that happen?"

"I can sure as hell try," I said, opening up a file I'd already started of successful women who were specifically looking for a man of means since they didn't want to be taken advantage of either. "How do you feel about trying out a handful of dates and seeing how well it goes?"

"I'd rather we start with a party." He placed both feet on the floor and leaned forward. "Like I said, I want to feel that spark the first time I meet them. I don't want to waste time if I know right away they aren't for me."

"Okaaaay, sure," I said slowly, trying not to think about the last time I'd put on a mixer for a client. Surely this one would go better, right?

Wrong. When would I ever learn? Because I was so very, very wrong.

CHAPTER 11

*A*fter Brix left the office, I glanced at my watch. It was early afternoon and I was starting to get anxious about the fact that I hadn't heard from anyone. Not Jax, Hollister, or Iris.

Standing up to pace, I hit Jax's number first. We weren't exactly in a place where we checked in with each other multiple times a day, but after the explosion the day before, I just felt the need to hear his voice.

"Hey, Marion. Everything okay? Did something happen?" he asked, concern coloring his tone.

"No, nothing happened. I'm fine. I just wanted to make sure you were okay." The tension in my shoulders eased just from hearing his voice.

"Yeah, I'm fine." His tone was softer now. The sound of a door closing came over the line, and all background noise ceased. I figured he must've stepped into his office. "The crew is pretty shaken up that someone did this, but they're eager to get the project back on track. We're just waiting for the inspectors to give us the go-ahead."

"That's good." I suddenly felt silly for being worried. I just couldn't shake off the sense of dread that had taken over as soon as my new client had walked out the door. Clearly, I needed something else to focus on while I waited to see if any of our leads panned out. "I have a new client," I blurted, not sure why I was bringing that up. New clients contacted me all the time.

"Oh? So you're in the office working?" He sounded surprised. "I'd have thought you'd be too preoccupied with everything else to work much."

"The coven is meeting tonight, and I'm waiting to hear from Hollister. I had to do something to keep my mind busy," I said, sounding defensive even to my own ears.

"Sure. Yeah. That makes sense," he said hesitantly. Then he blew out a breath. "I didn't mean anything by that, Marion. A lot has happened in the past couple of days. I hadn't even considered you'd go into work, but it makes sense that you did. You never were one for idle hands. Tell me about the new client."

"It's not important," I said, waving a dismissive hand even though he couldn't see me. "I really only called because I wanted to hear your voice. Like you said, a lot has happened the last couple of days, and I wanted to reassure myself that you're okay."

"I am. And, Marion?"

"Hmm?"

"I'm glad you called. I was worried about you, too." He paused for a moment. "I know you have the meeting with the coven later, but afterward, do you want to come to my house? I'll cook."

"Yes," I said immediately as that tingle in my spine came to life and warmth spread through my body. "I'll see you tonight."

Smiling to myself, I ended the call and scrolled until I found Hollister's number.

He answered on the first ring. "I haven't found anything," he huffed out. "Not one record of Kiera's car at any impound lot within a hundred miles. In fact, when I tried to run a search on her license plate number to see if there was anything that would be useful, there was no history of the number at all."

"What do you mean no history? How is that possible?" I frowned, trying to understand what that could mean.

"The only way it should be possible is if it's a fake plate. But I called Garrison. He said it must be a system error because he was with her when she registered the car."

"You think he's wrong? That it's not just a system error?" I guessed.

"Honestly, I don't know. But after that chaos spell, I think anything is possible. If someone wanted to make Kiera disappear, erasing her vehicle history with the DMV would certainly make it harder for anyone to find her car."

I had to admit that he could be on to something. "If that's true, what do we do now?"

His tone was stone cold when he said, "I'm going to run a trace on her name and see what records turn up. Her real name."

"You know her real name?" I asked, astonished. She'd told me she'd never tell anyone. It was too dangerous.

"No, but you do."

The implication was clear. He wanted me to confess what I knew. But that wasn't going to happen. "I'll do the check myself."

Hollister let out a growl of frustration. "Marion, you can't keep this secret. Not anymore. If we're going to find her, you're going to have to share what you know."

"Maybe." I wasn't stupid. It was true that we had a better chance of finding her if I shared more with Hollister, but I also knew Kiera absolutely would not want Garrison targeted, and that's exactly what would happen if I spilled my guts to his brother. If anyone found out Hollister was digging, they'd go after Garrison and force Hollister to choose. Kiera had been more than clear about various scenarios over the years. I wouldn't betray her trust now. "But not now. I'll find a way to do a background check on both of her names and let you know if anything comes up."

"Marion!" Celia popped into the office a second after she called my name. Her hair was windblown, and her face was pinched with worry. "You have to come now. It's Kennedy."

"That's not—" Hollister started, but I cut him off.

"Sorry, Hollister. I have to go." I ended the call without an explanation and turned to Celia. "What's going on? Is he hurt?"

"Not yet. But if he keeps hanging around that jackass, he probably will be. He's at Sky's The Limit, and Skyler is seconds from calling the police."

"For what?" I asked, already grabbing my keys and wallet.

"Shoplifting." Celia disappeared, leaving me with more questions than answers.

"Dammit!" I hurried out the door, anger all but consuming me. Shoplifting? Was Celia serious? I couldn't imagine Kennedy doing something like that. Especially since he'd left my home so that he wouldn't feel like he was taking advantage of me. But the truth was I'd only met the young man a few weeks ago. I didn't actually know if this was unusual for him.

As I hurried down Main Street, I wondered if maybe his relationship with his parents was strained for more reasons than just his sexual identity. Did it matter? No. Absolutely not.

Whatever Kennedy had done in the past, it didn't excuse his parents' rejection just because he was dating another man.

My heart sank when I saw the police cruiser outside of Sky's The Limit. It wasn't that I blamed Skyler. If someone had shoplifted at my high-end designer store, I'd probably call the cops, too. I'd just been hoping to work something out before things escalated that far.

The store's front door was propped open, and there were half a dozen people inside. I spotted Kennedy immediately. His head was down, and his wrists were in handcuffs at his back.

My heart ached at the image. In just a few short weeks, I'd come to really care for the young man. It was painful to see him detained by the police.

Celia was hovering near the male police officer who had a name tag that read *J. Stone* on his uniform. She was making noise about it not being Kennedy's fault and that another man had been in the store and forced Kennedy to stuff the goods in his backpack.

"Ma'am," the police officer said, sounding impatient. "I can't take a statement from a ghost."

"Then check the security cameras! Ask Kennedy. He'll tell you," Celia insisted.

All eyes landed on the tall, thin man in handcuffs.

Kennedy, with his head still bowed, didn't glance up at any of us.

I quickly walked over to him. "Is that true? Did someone force you to do this?"

"It's true," Celia insisted. "I saw that douche cast a spell, and before I knew it"—she waved an impatient hand—"this happened."

A spell? Dread coiled in my belly. Had someone cursed

89

Kennedy? I couldn't dismiss Celia's claims. After all, I'd been the victim of a curse recently myself.

Kennedy's head jerked up. "Marion, I…" The words seemed to get stuck in his throat as panic filled his blue eyes.

"You don't need to say anything right now," I said, placing a soft hand on his shoulder as I turned to Skyler, the owner of the shop, who also happened to be Gigi's neighbor. "What happened here?"

"The alarm went off when he tried to leave." Skyler frowned as he eyed Kennedy. "We found a thousand dollars' worth of clothes and skin care in his backpack." The shop owner's expression turned puzzled as if he was trying to work something out. "Do you know this kid?"

"Yes. He's dating my son, Ty. Kennedy just moved up to Premonition Pointe recently."

Skyler swept his gaze over Kennedy, his frown deepening.

"Marion, you don't—" Kennedy tried again, but I held my hand up.

"Can I talk to you for a second?" I asked Skyler. "In private?"

"Ma'am," a female police officer said. "We have a job to do. Can't this wait?"

"No," I insisted, squinting to read her last name. Matson. I committed that to memory and then turned my attention back to Skyler. "Just a quick minute?"

He hesitated for a moment and then gave me a short nod. We walked out onto the sidewalk so that we could still see what was going on in the store while we talked.

"Listen, Skyler," I said, hoping I didn't sound too desperate. "I know this is a lot to ask, but Kennedy has had a really rough few weeks. There's a reason he moved up here other than to be with Ty. After he came out to his parents…" I shook my head.

None of that was my story to tell, but I needed something to keep Skyler from sending him to jail. "It wasn't good. And I'm not excusing what he did. Not at all. But if Celia is right and he was spelled into doing this, then I just feel like if he's arrested right now, he's not going to recover."

Skyler stared inside at the police, who seemed to be completely ignoring Kennedy while Celia waved her hands and continued to try to get them to listen to her story. She wasn't always the most reliable when recounting events, but she did seem pretty adamant about what she'd seen. In fact, she looked frustrated, and a frustrated Celia was pretty rare. I was inclined to believe her story. "It doesn't make sense to me why Kennedy would steal the dresses that were in his backpack," Skyler said.

"Dresses?" I asked, more than a little surprised. "I know the kids these days are crossing gender lines with their fashion choices, but so far, I haven't seen any indication that he might be interested in that. Ty either, for that matter."

"The dresses are far too small for him," Skyler said, tapping his index finger on his lips. "And the face products aren't suited for Kennedy's skin profile. That ghost might be right. That other guy could have compelled him to put those items in his backpack. I'll need to check the security cameras."

"Can you do that now?" I asked hopefully. "Before they haul Kennedy away?"

"Yeah." He nodded decisively and swept back into the store.

But before Skyler could pull up his security system on the computer, the cops were already moving Kennedy toward the door.

"You'll get a notice of the hearing," Matson said. "Unless he pleads out."

"Wait. Hearing?" I said, panic taking over.

"His bail will likely be set in the morning." The cop pushed Kennedy toward the door and barked, "Move."

"Wait!" Skyler called, waving his hands, his expression pinched with worry. "I don't want to press charges. Let's just chalk this all up to a misunderstanding."

The two police officers looked at each other, an unspoken communication happening between them. The woman tightened her grip on Kennedy's arm. "I really think we should work this out down at the station."

Skyler narrowed his eyes at her. "I don't see how there's anything to work out. I appreciate your time in coming down here, but it appears I've made a mistake. I'd appreciate it if you'd release Kennedy, please."

Again, the two officers shared a look. J. Stone shrugged one shoulder and then Matson sighed and released Kennedy from the cuffs. Matson leaned in close to Kennedy's ear. "I'll be keeping an eye on you, you little punk."

I wanted to snarl for her to just leave, but I held myself in check. Escalating the situation wasn't going to help anyone. We were all silent while the officers departed. Once they drove off, Skyler turned to Kennedy with his hands on his hips and said, "Listen, honey, you have some explaining to do."

Kennedy stared at him with his eyes wide and his Adam's apple bobbing as his mouth worked but no words came out.

"You can start with a thank you," Skyler said. "And then we can work out payment."

"Payment?" Kennedy asked, his eyes darting to the register area and the pile of clothes that had been left there.

"You're going to work off this infraction," Skyler said. "So how about we get started? There's a shipment in the back that needs to be unpacked and inventoried." He reached for an invoice and then handed it to Kennedy. "Check everything in, and then I'll show you how to tag everything."

Kennedy stood there for a moment, just holding the invoice with a stunned look on his face. "Um, thank you for getting me released."

"You're welcome." Skyler's voice was cool and unforgiving. "Just don't make me regret my decision. Keep your distance from that guy you came in here with. He's trouble. If there's one thing I've learned in life, it's that hanging around with shady people only brings you down. And then one day, you find yourself in the middle of a shitshow, bound with handcuffs while they bolt and leave you holding the bag without ever looking back. Do you understand what I'm telling you?"

The younger man nodded once before turning to me. "Marion, I didn't mean to get you caught up in this."

Celia let out a guffaw from behind him. "Turns out you shouldn't hang out with losers, especially when you have someone like Marion on your side. Holy effing idiot on a stick."

Kennedy stiffened and promptly slammed his mouth shut.

"Celia," I said with a sigh. "I appreciate the heads up. But how about you let me handle this from here?"

"Oh, I see," she said dramatically. "It was fine when I was just a watchdog, but now that I have opinions on shit, you're done, huh? Well, if you're interested in hearing about the douchebucket who is responsible for all this, you can ask me. Until then, I'm going to go climb Danny like a tree."

"Have fun," Skyler called as the ghost disappeared again.

"I'll just go get to work," Kennedy said so quietly I almost didn't hear him.

"Wait," I said and glanced at Skyler. "We'll be just a minute. There are a few things we need to straighten out."

Skyler nodded, and I slipped my arm through Kennedy's to guide him further into the store. We stopped near a display of skin care products where we were far enough away to have a private conversation but still within Skyler's sightline.

"What happened here?" I asked without any preamble.

Kennedy sucked in a long breath and shook his head. "I don't really know. One minute I was checking out the sale rack of upcycled jeans, and then my head started to spin as if I were going to pass out. I remember clutching one of the racks before my roommate said we had to go. On the way out, the alarm went off and Vince bolted. I don't know how that stuff got into my backpack."

I raised a skeptical eyebrow. "Seriously? You don't know? You don't remember stuffing them in there?"

"I'm not a thief," he said defiantly, finally showing me a little backbone.

"I never thought you were," I said honestly. "Who's Vince?"

"He's just a guy who offered me a couch until I find my own place."

"Just some guy?" I asked, my tone incredulous. "You just went home with some guy? Some guy who may have compelled you to steal from Skyler?"

He glanced away and shuffled his feet. "I needed somewhere to stay. I didn't know he'd do... this."

"You're staying with me. Understood?" My mom voice had come out in full force. It wasn't one I used often, but there was no way I was letting Kennedy couch surf with strangers, especially ones who compelled him to shoplift and then ran at the first hint of trouble.

"With Ty gone, I don't think—"

"Stop thinking," I said. "This isn't about Ty anymore. This is about you and me and the fact that I care what happens to you. If you can couch surf with some stranger, then you can stay in the apartment over my garage. Where you won't be cursed, or spelled, or coerced to do anything other than be a responsible human."

He raised his head, met my gaze, and nodded once.

"Good. When you're done here, you'll come home and we'll go over the house rules. Got it?"

"Yeah."

I reached out and squeezed his hand. "I know the situation with your parents has been challenging and you're going through a lot right now, but don't let all of that color your judgment. Ty and I care about you. Whatever is going on between you and Ty is your business. I won't interfere. Just try to remember that I'm here, I care, and I am happy to provide a safe landing if you're willing to accept my help."

He swallowed hard, and tears shone in his eyes as he quickly pulled me into a tight hug. When he pulled back, the tears were gone, and his voice was rough when he said, "Thank you, Mama Marion."

My heart swelled with love for him. I had no doubt that he was a good kid who was just having trouble finding his place in the world. Hopefully with a little stability, he'd find what he needed.

As Kennedy walked into the back room, clutching the inventory list, I joined Skyler at the counter.

"Here," Skyler said, pointing at the computer screen. "See that?"

I squinted at the pixilated picture. "What am I looking at?"

"Oh. This is the blown-up version. Here." He tapped a few keys and the entire frame came into focus. All I could see was a tattooed hand on Kennedy's shoulder. "Look at that spark." He blew up the picture again, revealing a silver outline clinging to the tattooed fingers. "That's definitely some sort of magic."

My mouth went dry as Celia's version of events was confirmed. That had to be Vince's hand, and he was certainly wielding some sort of magic. My hands balled into fists at what that bastard had done. He'd almost ruined Kennedy's life, all for a couple of dresses and some high-end skin care.

Skyler tapped the screen again, skipping a few frames. "See that? It's one of the dresses we found in the backpack." One more stroke of the key revealed Kennedy's lean frame. He was holding the dress, but he was standing stiffly, staring straight ahead as if in a trance. The tattooed hands held out the backpack as Kennedy gave one barely noticeable nod before stuffing the dress into the pack. The tattooed guy zipped it up and handed it back to Kennedy. "The video doesn't exactly prove that Kennedy didn't know what he was doing, but it's obvious to me that magic was involved. There's also the fact that when I asked to check his backpack after the alarms went off, he wasn't concerned at all. And when I found the dresses, he was clearly surprised. Unless he's one hell of an actor, I'm putting the blame squarely on that jackass with the tattoos, whoever he is."

"Kennedy said his name is Vince. Just some guy who was letting Kennedy couch surf," I said.

"Sounds like Kennedy needs to find better friends," Skyler said with a sniff. "Maybe working here until the debt is paid off will teach him to be more discerning about who he associates with."

"Agreed." I glanced at the door that led to the back room and then back at Skyler. "Thank you for the way you handled this. You have no idea how much I appreciate it."

He placed his hand on my forearm and squeezed gently. "Don't worry about it." There was true compassion in Skyler's expression when he added, "I was a little bit like Kennedy at one point in my life. When my parents rejected me, I made a lot of bad choices before I figured out that self-acceptance was the answer. I'm happy to give him a chance. As long as he doesn't take advantage of me, then we'll get along fine."

I almost snorted my incredulous reply, but held myself in check. "I have a feeling that the last thing he'd do is take advantage of you. The reason he's in this mess in the first place is because he was determined *not* to take advantage of me."

"That's how he ended up couch surfing?"

"Yep. Hopefully that's behind him now." I gave Skyler a hug, thanked him one more time, and then headed back to the office.

CHAPTER 12

$\mathcal{M}$y house was dark when I pulled into my driveway a few hours later. I had just enough time to change and then head over to the coven circle. Frowning, I glanced around for Tandy's car. It wasn't in the driveway or anywhere on the street. Usually she let me know if she was going somewhere. Not that she needed to check in with me. She was an adult after all. Still, things had been unsettling the past few weeks. I just wanted to know my people were safe and accounted for.

As I was walking in the door, I was already fishing my phone out of my pocket to text her, but before I pulled up her name, I spotted a note in Tandy's handwriting on the table where I always left my keys.

Marion, got a call about an emergency at the studio. Had to head back down to LA. I sent a text but didn't hear back. Chat soon. T.

I quickly scanned my phone for the alleged text but didn't find anything. I hadn't gotten a message from her since a few days before when she'd asked if I needed anything from the store. I quickly sent a reply to tell her I was sorry she had to go but to call me when she got home safely.

Thirty minutes later, I was back in my car and headed to the coven circle. It seemed I was there so often these days that I felt sort of like an honorary member.

Hollister was waiting for me next to his BMW. His entire body was tense and his voice wary when he spoke. "There's been a development."

My body turned cold. "What happened?" I glanced around, looking for the coven members' cars, but I didn't see any of them.

"Garrison got a letter in the mail, supposedly from Kiera. She asked him not to look for her."

"You don't think it was from her." It was a statement, not a question.

"I don't see how it can be considering it's a Dear John letter. Kiera would never do that to Garrison, especially while he's battling cancer. That's not the woman I know." Hollister started pacing back and forth. "Someone forced her to write it. Surely it was the people who abducted her, right?"

I nodded, an ache forming in my stomach. "If they went through the trouble to send Garrison the letter, then they know about him. And likely you, too," I said, suddenly feeling vulnerable. Had they been watching us this entire time? Did they know I was helping him look for Kiera?

"They certainly do. Which means he's in danger." His expression turned determined. "I can't stay here much longer. I need to get back to Garrison."

I'd expect nothing less from Hollister. If there was one thing that wasn't up for debate, it was how much he loved his brother. "Then let's get moving." I gestured for him to take the path toward the coven circle. Just because I didn't see any cars, that didn't mean that none of the coven members had arrived yet.

We walked in silence, and halfway to the bluff I got the strange feeling that I was being watched. I automatically reached into my purse and wrapped my hand around the dagger that I now carried with me everywhere. Magic tingled at both the base of my spine and in my fingertips that gripped the dagger.

I had no idea what triggered that magic response at the base of my spine. Was it the dagger? Or was it the other way around? Was my magic triggering the weapon? This was all new to me, and honestly, it frightened me a little. I just wasn't sure how to deal with it.

"Where are they?" Hollister asked when we got to the circle.

I checked the time on my phone. "This isn't right. They should have been here twenty minutes ago. Surely they didn't show up and leave because we are late, right?"

"I've been at the head of that trail since ten minutes before the hour. I didn't see anyone," he said.

"Dammit," I said, sucking in a sharp breath as I checked my phone. The last message I'd received was one from Iris letting me know the coven would be there tonight. I sent a quick text asking where she was.

No response.

That was unusual. Iris was always quick to reply back. She hadn't come into work that afternoon. Not that I'd expected her to, being that it was Sunday. That didn't always stop her though. The woman was just as determined as I was to make Miss Matched Midlife Dating Agency a success. My memory kicked into gear, reminding me that she'd mentioned something about having lunch with Gigi and Carly. Maybe they'd lost track of time?

After a few moments when there was still no response, I hit Iris's number. All I got was a busy signal. "What the hell?" I stared at the phone as if it could give me answers. "It's a busy signal. Shouldn't it have just gone straight to voice mail?"

"Sounds like a service issue," he said. "Let me try."

I rattled off the number and stared down the trail, willing a coven member to appear. No such luck.

Hollister shook his head. "I'm getting the busy signal, too."

I quickly scrolled through my contacts and tried Gigi next.

Busy signal.

After I'd worked my way through the four remaining coven members, I let out another curse and stared blindly out at the churning ocean. "Something's not right."

"I think that's fairly obvious," Hollister said.

I wanted to rage and scream at him for being an insufferable asshole, but truthfully, it was the whole situation I really wanted to rage and scream at. It was inconceivable that all six of the coven members would stand us up. Add in the fact that it was impossible to reach them by phone, and I was certain that they'd been victims of foul play. Fear crawled over my skin. Had Kiera's ex found them? It was the only thing that made sense. If he'd learned they were helping me… I shook my head, clearing away the troubling thoughts. We had to focus.

"There's nothing to do but go see if we can find them." I started back toward the path, but Hollister caught my hand, stopping me.

"Wait." He held out a butterfly broach that I hadn't seen in a few years. It was one I knew well, as it was half of a pair that had belonged to my grandmother. I'd kept one and given the other to Kiera the day she'd moved out of my house and into her own apartment.

"This is what you brought to do the finding spell?" I asked.

He fingered the broach, caressing it lightly. "She wears it all the time."

My heart started to ache for the woman I'd known. For whatever she was going through. For Garrison and Hollister, her new family. I placed my hand over his, trapping the butterfly between our palms. "We'll find her."

Magic started to tingle at the base of my spine until it sparked out of my fingertips and engulfed our still-joined hands.

I was thrown into a whirlwind of chaos. Visions flooded my mind, all of them distorted as if they were coming through like something resembling a Picasso painting. A vision of Kiera broke through, her nose too large, one green eye bigger than the other, peering right at me as she gave me a twisted smile. Her mouth opened and words jumbled out.

Stop. Let me be. I'm happy here. It's over. Move on.

The words continued to flow, but a single large teardrop slid down her distorted, angular face. Pain sluiced through my heart, making me feel as if someone had struck me right in the chest with a dagger. My throat clogged and I couldn't breathe.

Panic took over, and my entire body started to shake.

"I'm trapped! I'll never get out of here! Keep Garrison safe!" The words exploded from my lips, but they weren't mine. They'd come from someone else.

Kiera.

"Marion!" Hollister shook me, his face right in front of mine. "I'm right here. Look at me. That's right. Look at me."

I blinked rapidly, trying to clear the confusing images still swirling in my brain. All of the coven members appeared, each of them scowling and shaking their heads as if they were angry. Then there was only Ty and Jax, both of them begging me to stop looking for Kiera. They were worried. Ty's eyes filled with tears as he started to fade away, and Jax shook his head sadly as his shoulders slumped right before he disappeared, leaving me with nothing but a deep-seated emptiness consuming my body and soul.

"Marion!" Hollister held my shoulders, gently shaking me out of my fever dream. "Please, just look at me."

My eyes focused on the man in front of me, all the chaos finally gone. I tried to open my mouth to say something, to explain my visions to him, but before I could, a bright light blinded me, making me take a step back as I threw my hands up, shielding my eyes.

Hollister let out a grunt and then dropped to the ground, his body appearing lifeless at my feet.

"Oh my gods! Hollister!" I cried, bending down to check on him. I pressed my fingers to his wrist and let out a tiny sigh of relief when I felt a strong pulse still beating. But when I peered down at his face, his expression was slack and it was clear he was unconscious.

"He won't wake for a while," a deep voice said from behind me.

I jumped to my feet and spun around, my hand already clutching the dagger that I kept in my bag.

"I wouldn't try it if I were you," the man said. He was hidden by shadows, making it impossible for me to make out his features.

"Try what, exactly?" I demanded, sounding a lot more confident than I actually felt. My heart was racing, and I was fairly certain that once the adrenaline wore off I'd be shaking like a leaf.

"Stabbing me with that dagger." He lifted his arm and swept it to the side, sending a force of magic that slammed right into my arm, paralyzing it. The dagger fell from my hand as my arm hung limply at my side.

I stared at my useless arm, fear silencing me as I realized I was all but defenseless against this strange man.

"Now that I have your attention, you might want to listen carefully," he said in a tone filled with self-satisfaction.

I glared in his general direction as I clutched my useless arm. If I wasn't certain he'd render me completely paralyzed, I'd have already used my good hand to grab the dagger and hurl it in his direction.

"Your rebellious nature is writing checks you can't cash," he snarled.

"What do you want from me?" I demanded, suddenly so furious I was about one second from launching myself at him, determined to scratch his eyes out.

"Kiera sent me to deliver a message."

"Yeah, Kiera's the one who sent you," I scoffed. "Do you really think I'm going to believe that, especially after you knocked out my friend?"

"It's better if Hollister hears this message from you." The man's voice was cold, void of all emotion.

"Just spit it out," I demanded, knowing there was no chance of escape until I heard whatever messaged he'd come to deliver.

"Kiera wants you to stop looking for her. She's made her choices and doesn't want anyone else involved. Specifically you and Garrison Crooner."

I continued to glare at the shadowed man even though the base of my spine was tingling, making me believe that he was telling the truth. Everything I knew about Kiera told me that if she thought we were in danger, she'd sacrifice herself to be sure those she cared about were safe. "Okay. I've heard her request. But I can't promise I'll comply."

Why had I said that? It was probably because I couldn't stand to be intimidated. But that didn't negate the fact that I should have kept my big mouth shut.

"I'd think twice about that, Marion Matched. It sure would be a shame if anything happened to that father of yours. Or Ty. Or even that sad young man who is staying with you again. You wouldn't want that, would you? I'm sure your Aunt Lucy would rather we keep her out of this too."

A growl rumbled from the back of my throat.

The man gave a soft chuckle. "You are a feisty one, aren't you?"

"What did you do to the coven?" I demanded, my entire body vibrating with fury now. "If you hurt any one of them, I swear to the goddess—"

"Relax," he said impatiently, cutting me off. "Your *coven* will be free to play amateur sleuths the next time they get a hankering for lighting their candles. Just as long as they don't light them for Kiera. Understand?"

I ground my teeth together, unable to even form words.

"I can see you're having trouble accepting Kiera's request," he said almost conversationally. After a slight pause, he added, "Let me make myself perfectly clear. Drop the search for Kiera or everyone you know and love will be in danger. We'll come for every last one of them before we finally neutralize you."

I desperately wanted to scream. To tell the faceless man to fuck off into the sun. To march him back to the cliff and throw him over to the rocks below. But before I could act on any of those impulses, the man swirled his long trench coat and then disappeared into the mist, appearing to teleport right before my eyes.

The air felt heavy with tainted magic. The kind that made my skin crawl. The man who'd threatened me was heavily into illegal magic, though if he was connected to law enforcement, there was little chance he'd ever be charged for his crimes.

Hollister stirred at my feet, and I belatedly dropped to my knees, quickly pressing my palm to his cheek. My other arm still hung limply at my side, and I briefly wondered how long it'd be out of commission.

"Hollister?" I asked, praying that he'd woken.

But he didn't move. And his breathing was shallow, his pulse thready.

"Dammit, Hollister," I cried. "You need to wake up now. Do you hear me?"

Silence.

Tears of pure frustration burned the backs of my eyes, but I quickly blinked them away, unwilling to let anyone see me frazzled. For all I knew that mysterious man in the cloak was hanging back, just watching me. Showing weakness wasn't an option.

"Hollister," I said again, staring at his face in earnest. "Come on, man. We have to get out of here."

When he continued to lie lifelessly on the ground, that familiar flutter of panic started to take over again.

"No. This isn't happening," I said to no one as I shook my head. "I will not leave you here. You will wake up and walk away from here under your own steam. Do you hear me?" I ran my hand down one of his lifeless arms, and the moment my fingers touched his hand, magic burst from me, driving straight into his palm.

Hollister bolted upright, blinked away the confusion, and then focused right on me. "Marion? What happened?"

I was so overwhelmed with the fact that Hollister appeared

to be okay, I practically lunged for him and caught him in a tight one-armed hug.

"Marion?" he asked again, though this time he was much quieter, talking to me as if he was afraid that I'd bolt. "What's wrong? What happened?"

"I'm..." I shook my head, trying to clear my thoughts. I needed to tell him about the warning, but at that moment, all I cared about was that he was awake and appeared to be okay despite the magical attack he'd suffered. I stood and held my hand out to him. "Come on. We need to go."

He climbed to his feet, only swaying once or twice until he found his balance.

It was good enough for me. I clutched his hand and said, "Let's go."

CHAPTER 13

"*W*hat happened back there?" Hollister asked as I climbed into his BMW.

With my bad arm, driving wasn't exactly safe. My SUV would have to be left behind. "Do you remember anything?"

"Just that you had some sort of vision and then…" He shook his head. "Nothing until I found myself on the ground with you staring at me with wide, panicked eyes."

"There certainly was good reason for that," I said with a sigh. "We need to head to Gigi's house."

"I think I need to get you to a healer. That arm of yours—"

"It'll be fine," I snapped, though he had a point. An ache had started at my shoulder and was making its way toward my elbow. But I still didn't have any control over the limb. It was completely useless. Maybe after I was certain everyone I cared about was safe and sound, then I'd worry about my injury. "Right now, you need to know about the man who knocked you unconscious."

He turned and blinked at me, making no move to start the engine. "I was attacked?"

What did he think, that he'd just passed out? "Yeah. The lump on your noggin is the reason you're likely battling a headache right now."

His hands tightened on the steering wheel. His voice was low and full of quiet rage when he said, "Tell me everything."

Needing to feel somewhat in control, I reached into my bag and grabbed the dagger I'd desperately wanted while dealing with the mysterious stranger. Magic tickled my fingertips and then skittered over my skin. My limp arm started to tingle, and I let out a small gasp as I quickly pulled the dagger out of the bag and pressed it into my other palm. The magic sparked and crackled over my hand until my fingers curled around the handle all on their own. The magic intensified, engulfing my entire arm. What started off as a warm tingle quickly turned into searing pain, making me cry out from the agony.

"Marion?" Hollister reached for me, but as soon as he touched me, he gasped and yanked his hand back, clutching it to his chest. "Holy shit. What's happening?"

I shook my head, truly not understanding why the magic had taken over. All I knew was that if I wanted the pain to stop, I had to drop the damned dagger. Only I couldn't. My grip was out of my control. There was nothing I could do except grit my teeth and pray for the magic to release me.

Hollister shifted in his seat, appearing restless to do something. Anything. But every time he got close to the dagger, the magic intensified, only making my pain worse.

"Stop," I gritted out. "Just... wait."

There was a terrible silence in the car as we both stared at my magic-engulfed arm, waiting for something, anything, to happen.

Finally, Hollister said, "Fuck this. I'm taking you to a healer."

Before I could say anything, he had the car in gear and peeled away from the curb, heading to town.

"Gigi can help," I said. "Go there."

"Marion, this is serious. We need professional help," he said, pressing into the gas as he took a corner.

My entire body lurched toward the passenger door. There was no way to stop the impact, and my already compromised arm slammed into the window. The magic blinked out and my fingers uncurled from the dagger, causing it to drop to the floorboard.

"Jesus, Marion." Hollister jerked the car to a stop on the side of the road.

I glared at him. "What are you doing? Don't stop. Get to Gigi's house. I need to check on the coven members."

"But your arm?" His expression was full of concern.

Normally I would've appreciated that he cared, but I'd lost every bit of my patience. "I'm fine, Hollister. Just go. Please." I rolled my shoulder, showing him that I would live and that there was no need to waste any more time.

He blew out a long breath. "Hell. Could this day get any longer?"

"It's not over yet," I said and flexed my hand, managing to hold back a wince. I wasn't back to normal, but at least my arm wasn't dead weight anymore, nor was it screaming in pain from the magic. Now it was just sore, and I was certain that with a few pain killers I'd manage just fine until it healed.

Rain started to fall lightly, but it wasn't long before it picked up, splattering the windshield with large rapid-fire drops. I leaned forward, squinting into the darkness. It seemed fitting that we'd end the day with a downpour. It was just that kind of evening.

"Turn here," I said, gesturing to the street that would take us to Gigi and Sebastian's beach house.

"Your friend lives here?" he asked a moment later when I told him to pull over. Hollister stood under an umbrella, holding my door open while he squinted at the walkway that was covered in pristinely manicured foliage, including a jasmine-covered arbor that led to the doorway.

"Yep. She has a way with plants," I said and walked right past him and onto the porch. The house seemed to sense me, and I felt a connection to the place in a way I never had before. Like something or someone was alive and keeping an eye out for me. Normally that kind of feeling would freak me out, but in this case, it just felt comforting.

Hollister, on the other hand, seemed to be eyeing everything with extreme suspicion.

"Relax," I said and pushed the button for the doorbell.

A series of chimes went off, sounding a lot like *The Addams Family* theme song.

Hollister took a step back.

I lifted my head and laughed for what seemed like the first time in weeks.

"Marion?" Gigi said when she opened the door a second later. "I thought you'd left town?"

I rushed her, wrapping my arms around her small body and hugging her tightly.

Gigi let out a small nervous laugh as she hugged me back. "This is unexpected, but I guess a spontaneous hug from a good friend is a nice little surprise.

Still hugging her tightly, afraid to let go for fear she'd disappear right before my eyes, I said, "I thought something had happened to you and the rest of the coven. When you didn't show up at the coven circle, I naturally thought the worst."

"What?" Gigi pulled away and then blinked up at me. "You canceled the coven meeting. Why did you think we'd be there?"

"I didn't cancel it," I said.

She frowned, her forehead creasing with her troubled expression. "I don't understand. We got a text..." She turned around and walked back into the house, waving for us to follow.

I gladly put down the umbrella and followed her inside, only stopping long enough to take off my shoes and hang up my jacket.

"In here," Gigi called from the depths of her living room.

I followed her voice, finding her sitting next to a big picture window that looked out over the Premonition Pointe Bay. Even though it was still raining, the moon was shining down, creating a shimmer of silver moonlight on the bay. Again, I got that sense that the effect of the unusual occurrence of the visible moon in the rain was there just for me. To comfort me or let me know that even though I was in the middle of the storm, a light would always guide me home. I shook my head slightly. Was I so desperate for a sign that Kiera would be okay that I was making up omens to make myself feel better?

I thought for certain that was the case, but when my spine started to tingle with magic, I knew it wasn't just wishful thinking. I was certain that whatever else was going on, the moon was there to give me hope. To keep me from giving up. It was the light in the storm and exactly what I needed in that moment.

Gigi held out her phone. "That's the text that was sent to all of us... except Iris. I assumed she got her own."

It read: *Kiera got in touch with Garrison. No need to search for her anymore. The finding spell is canceled.*

"You even answered us back when we asked about Kiera. Do you not remember any of this?" Gigi asked.

I shook my head slowly. "No. And we didn't hear from Kiera. Not exactly," I explained. "Garrison got a Dear John letter, but I don't believe for one moment that she wanted to send that letter."

"This is bad," Gigi said as she wrung her hands. Gigi had been a victim of domestic violence herself. This had to be stirring up old issues for her. Before I could say anything, she straightened her shoulders and stared me right in the eye. "We all know that letter was bullshit. What we need to focus on right now is those messages. If you didn't write them, who did?"

This was the part I was dreading the most. Acknowledging that everyone I loved was in danger. "It's definitely Kiera's ex."

"Her ex found you?" Gigi asked with a gasp.

I nodded. "And the coven, too, since you all got messages that weren't from me. Can you get the rest of the coven over here?" I asked, even though I was dead on my feet. "I need to see for myself that they are okay, or I won't ever stop imagining the worst happening."

"Yeah." Gigi sent out a message to the rest of the coven members, and even though they too were confused, all of them accepted and promised to be there shortly.

I took a seat, leaned my head back, and closed my eyes. I'd wait until the entire coven was there to explain what had happened with the mysterious stranger. I just needed a moment to wrap my head around it.

The next thing I knew, I woke suddenly to Hollister and Sebastian arguing, the two of them toe to toe in Gigi's living room.

CHAPTER 14

"*N*o way. Giving up on Kiera isn't an option," Hollister said through clenched teeth. His fists were curled into balls, and he was so angry he was practically vibrating.

"She's not who she represented herself to be," Sebastian shot back. "Putting the entire coven right in the middle of that minefield isn't an option."

"Sebastian," Gigi said, placing a light hand on his arm. "Let's take a breath and—"

Her significant other placed his hand over hers and then pulled her into him, tucking her under his arm. "It's too dangerous, G. I know that when you learned she was a victim of domestic violence you had to do whatever you could to help. But now that we know she's a former agent for the Paranormal Task Force and was indicted for manslaughter, it seems her story was completely fabricated. Butting in on this could land the entire coven into a legal nightmare, not to mention it's dangerous as hell. Promise me you'll stay far away from this."

I stared at Sebastian and Gigi, my mouth hanging open as I tried to process what Sebastian had just said. *Magical Task Force agent? Indicted for manslaughter?*

"We can't just write off Kiera," Hollister insisted. "The woman I know isn't a criminal. Or a murderer."

"*Murderer?*" I finally got out as I perched on the edge of the couch. "Someone needs to tell me what's going on, because I feel like I woke up to an alternate reality."

Everyone turned my direction, obviously just noticing I was awake.

Gigi quickly hurried over and sat next to me. "Sebastian got the fingerprint results back from the dagger."

"Okay," I said, my gaze boring into Sebastian's. "What did you find?"

Sebastian took a step away from Hollister and moved to sit on the coffee table in front of me. "The prints belong to Desiree Ciaràn Hopkins."

I nodded.

"You knew her real name." Hollister said. It was a statement, not a question. "I thought so."

"I did. It's one of the things she forbade me to talk about to anyone." I stared past Hollister as I added, "For everyone else's safety."

"For her own is more like it," Sebastian said, his tone ice-cold.

"Explain," I demanded.

Sebastian ran a frustrated hand through his dark hair and started to pace the living room. "We actually got the results of the prints back yesterday."

"And you didn't call Marion?" Gigi asked, her expression pinched in concern.

"No." He shook his head. "Because there was absolutely nothing on her. It was as if her entire history had been wiped from all of the assessable data bases."

Sebastian was a high-powered lawyer and had access to searchable databases that weren't available to the general public.

"At first I thought maybe she was part of a witness protection program," Sebastian continued. "But when the private investigator did a deeper dive, he found evidence that she'd worked for the Magical Task Force. And as you may know, we have contacts there. That's when we got confirmation that she was an agent and has been on the run since she was indicted for manslaughter." Sebastian picked up a file that was lying on top of a credenza and handed it to me. "Kiera's story about leaving an abusive ex is fiction."

I stared down at the unopened file, my entire body cold with pure dread. Was what Sebastian said true? Had I been played by a savvy Magical Task Force agent who was on the run? It sure explained why she was so adamant that I never go to law enforcement if she ever went missing. If she decided she needed to run again, she wouldn't want to leave a trail behind. Bile crawled up the back of my throat. Had I been party to harboring a fugitive?

"I don't believe it," Hollister said, crossing his arms over his chest. "I know Kiera. She'd never lie to Garrison about such a thing."

I gave him a flat stare. "Is that what you really think? She's been lying to him about her identity this entire time. What makes you think this couldn't have all just been an elaborate story?" The words felt wrong coming out of my mouth, and my stomach turned at the thought of doubting the woman I'd grown to love. But with Sebastian's information, how could I just take what she'd told me at face value?

"I can't believe you're willing to throw away years of friendship without even giving her the benefit of the doubt," Hollister said, shaking his head and heading for the front door.

I stood. "Where are you going?"

"Home. I need to check on Garrison and decide where to go from here." He opened the door and strode out.

"Hollister, wait!" I ran after him, hurrying outside in the rain in my bare feet. He was already at his car when I caught up to him. "What makes you so sure that Kiera was telling me the truth, when she kept it from everyone else this whole time?"

"Because I know her heart," he said, staring past me into the drizzly night.

There was melancholy in his expression and for the first time, I started to wonder if he felt something more for Kiera than just brotherly love. "She can still have a good heart even if everything Sebastian said is true," I reasoned. "If she was indicted for manslaughter, that implies the death was accidental or at least not premeditated, right? We don't know the details. We don't know if she was a victim of the system or if she really did mess up and thought her only way out was to run."

He shrugged one shoulder. "Does it matter now? Are you really going to keep looking for her if her story was fabricated? Or will you wash your hands of everything and leave it up to the authorities to work out?"

I opened my mouth to speak, but then quickly closed it. I had no idea what I intended to do. But one thing I did know was that if Kiera was indicted by the Magical Task Force, then there wasn't much I could do for her. That was for lawyers and powerful witches within the system. Not a matchmaker with little knowledge of how to fight the law.

"That's what I thought." He pulled his door open. Just before he slipped into the driver's seat, he said, "Take care of yourself, Marion. And keep that dagger close. The connection you have to the magic will keep you safe if you let it."

I nodded and watched as he closed the door and drove into the night. With a sigh, I hurried back up the path to Gigi's house. I found her just inside the door, holding a towel and a hot cup of tea.

"Here," she said, handing me the tea. "It's infused with healing herbs. It should help that shoulder of yours. It did wonders for Hollister's headache."

"You gave him some, too?" I asked.

She nodded. "While you were snoozing on the couch." She gave me a gentle smile and wrapped the towel around my shoulders then led me back through the living room and into the kitchen. "Are you hungry? I can make you something to eat."

I frowned. Was I? I had no idea when I'd eaten last.

"Never mind. It's obvious you need something," she said. "I'll be right back."

I took a seat at the table and quickly texted Jax that the spell was a bust and I wasn't going to make it for dinner. Then I added that I'd call him when I got home to explain everything. With my arms folded in front of me, I put my head down, trying and failing to wipe away Hollister's look of disappointment as he'd gotten into his car. The truth was that I was disappointed, too. And also angry.

Why had that mysterious man shown up and told me to

stop looking for Kiera? Who was he? Someone from the Magical Task Force? If that was true, why didn't he just identify himself? Wouldn't it have been easier and more effective for the agency to inform me that she was a person of interest? Was she already in their custody or were they still looking for her? Was the mysterious man from the agency or someone else entirely? Had she sent him? The thought horrified me and I quickly dismissed it. Surely she wouldn't let anyone hurt Hollister, right?

There were too many questions that I had no hope of answering.

"Here," Gigi said.

I lifted my head and waited while she put a plate of what looked to be leftover ravioli in front of me.

"It's chicken and goat cheese," she said. "And here's the garlic bread. Wine?"

I shook my head. "Just water."

"You've got it." She poured a glass from a pitcher and handed it to me just as the doorbell rang.

"It's Iris," she said.

"How do you know?" I squinted toward the entryway, but with the lights on, there was no way to see through the side windows.

"The house told me," she said mysteriously and smiled as she practically floated toward the front door. Sure enough, when she opened it, Iris strode in. She quickly hugged Gigi and then made a beeline for me.

"Marion," she said, wrapping her arms around me from behind and giving me a hug. "Thank the gods you're okay. When Gigi called and told me what happened..." She hugged me tighter. "I'm just so relieved you're all right."

Gigi took a seat across from me while Iris sat to my right.

"A lot has happened tonight," Iris said.

I nodded. That certainly seemed true enough.

The doorbell rang again, and Sebastian opened it to reveal the rest of the coven. The other four women filed in, all of them subdued. Finally as they sat at the table, Hope pushed her dark hair back and asked, "What happened?"

"An agent from the Magical Task Force came to see me," Iris said at the same time I blurted, "I was attacked at the coven circle."

"What? Why?" I asked her.

"To warn me that we're stepping into something that could get us into real trouble," she said.

"Let's start with Marion's story," Sebastian said in his smooth lawyer voice.

Even though I desperately wanted to hear what the Magical Task Force agent told Iris, I nodded and did my best to recount the encounter. Seven pairs of eyes were trained on me as I explained how I'd never texted any of them about canceling the finding spell. That I'd been worried when they hadn't shown up, that my phone had been nothing but a busy signal, and finally the attack on Hollister and the mysterious man's warning to stop looking for Kiera.

"Someone attacked Hollister?" Carly asked, her eyes wide and full of worry. "Where is he? Is he all right?"

"He left not long ago to be with Garrison," I said. "He's okay. Just got a bump on the head."

"I gave him tea that helped with the headache," Gigi said. "He didn't appear to have a concussion."

"That's... insane," Joy said almost to herself.

Everyone was in agreement.

"Do you think it was Kiera's ex?" Grace Valentine asked,

reminding me that they hadn't been filled in on Sebastian's discovery.

I met Sebastian's gaze and gave him a slight nod, indicating that he should explain.

He nodded once. "We have reason to believe that Kiera was running from the law and not an abusive ex." He held up the report his PI had done on her. "It turns out she's a former agent for the Magical Task Force and is on the run after being indicted for manslaughter."

Joy let out a gasp as she covered her mouth. Then she slowly shook her head as her eyes widened. "My vision. The black SUV. Was that the authorities recovering her?"

"We don't know," I said, but it certainly was possible.

"Well, this backs up the visit I got today," Iris said with a tired sigh.

"What visit?" I asked her.

"I have a contact at the Magical Task Force. Someone I worked with and who came through for us when the town was cursed. Ginny Stevens."

Grace, Hope, and Joy all shared a look and then all three nodded at the same time.

"We remember her," Grace said.

"She showed up at my door late this afternoon and warned me that looking into Kiera's past was a really bad idea for me and Marion. She said that we were walking into a landmine and that things could get ugly fast." Iris turned to me. "Especially for you. She mentioned that if you didn't back off there could be charges for harboring a fugitive."

I pressed my hand to my throat and swallowed hard. "What else did she say?"

Iris shook her head. "Nothing. She told me that she shouldn't be here at all and that she was taking a risk even talking to me about it. But she said she knew I was above board and wanted to make sure I didn't walk into something unknowingly that would endanger me or my coven." She glanced around at her friends and then met my gaze. "I trust Ginny. She was a true professional when working on the curse that was cast on Premonition Pointe. If she says we should stay out of this, then I'm inclined to listen. Especially after what Sebastian found out."

"I just…" I started and then clamped my mouth closed. I could not sit there and ask my friends to do anything that would put them or their families in harm's way. If the Magical Task Force was involved and said Kiera was dangerous, then I had to listen to them, right?

"What is it?" Hope asked gently. "We know you care about Kiera. And I'm certain I speak for everyone when I say none of us would walk away from a friend in need. But—"

"I know. It sounds like Kiera played me. Or at the very least, lied to cover her own ass. But I really care for her, and none of this is making sense in regard to the woman I knew. It's just hard to reconcile, I guess."

Iris reached over and covered my hand with hers. Squeezing, she said, "Trust me when I say I understand that feeling of betrayal when it doesn't make any sense."

I nodded, recalling that her husband had been secretly involved with a drug runner and had been the reason she'd lost her mayorship. Because of him, she'd lost her marriage and her career at the same time. I hadn't lost anything… yet. But I might if I didn't let this go. "I'm sorry, Iris. I know this isn't anything like what you went through."

She pressed her lips into a thin line and shook her head. "Don't do that. A betrayal is a betrayal. Your trust is broken. I just wanted you to know that I understand."

"Thanks," I said.

Silence followed as we all seemed to sit with the fact that we were no longer going to be looking for Kiera.

Finally, Grace cleared her throat and said, "There's something I don't understand."

I raised my gaze to hers and waited.

"Who sent us the text that the finding spell was off? Obviously it wasn't you if you and Hollister went to the coven circle and were waiting for us," she said.

"I have no idea," I said, frowning. "Someone from the Magical Task Force, maybe?"

"I'd guess it was the same mysterious guy who attacked Hollister," Iris said. "He ambushed you two. I assume he didn't want us there to interrupt him."

I narrowed my eyes at her, trying to figure something out. "Gigi said you weren't in the text chain. How did you know the spell was off?"

"I got a text from you," she said, holding up her phone. "But it was at the same time that Ginny was warning me off, and I wanted to talk to you first before I told everyone else about her visit. I texted you and you said we'd talk tomorrow."

I glanced at her text chain and sure enough, it looked like I'd texted her. My stomach rolled with nausea. That was unsettling to say the least. "Is there a way to cleanse a phone?" I asked. "Kinda like doing a ritual to ask ghosts to leave, only something more of a magical cleanse?"

"Well, yeah. It's kinda like a smudging," Carly said. "We can do that if you want."

I had no idea if it would work, but I was all in. I put my phone in the middle of the table. "Let's do it."

The coven members all agreed and surrendered their phones.

Carly and Gigi put their heads together, and it wasn't long before the coven was standing in a circle, demanding that any residual magic be banished from our phones. With magic swirling in the air, I was certain that I saw a gray line of smoke escape from the devices and hover near an open window before it disappeared into the night.

CHAPTER 15

*T*he welcoming glow from my porch light nearly brought me to tears. It had been one hell of a day and the fact that someone, probably Jax, had thought to leave the light on for me was just enough to tear down the last of my defenses.

I took a moment to collect myself and then walked in to find Jax sitting on the couch holding a mug. "Hey," he said. "Hope you don't mind that I made myself at home. I figured after the evening you had, you could use a little support."

I gave him a grateful smile and noticed there was a half-empty tin of what looked to be shortbread cookies on the coffee table in front of him. "Was Aunt Lucy here?"

"Yes," Jax said, giving me a sheepish smile. "She brought your favorite. Lemon shortbread. Kennedy and I figured you'd need help finishing them off."

"Tonight, I could probably eat the entire tin all by myself," I said. "Good thing you two had a head start." I glanced around, noting that Kennedy was not in the living room. "Did Kennedy go to bed?"

"He did. In the guest room. He said something about needing a space free of Ty. I saw Tandy's note and figured since she'd left that was okay. Is it?"

"Of course," I said, frowning in the direction of the spare room. Ty was still in LA as far as I knew. I wondered what that was about.

"He told me what happened. All I can say is that he's embarrassed and very grateful for your help," Jax said.

I nodded. "Today was… a lot."

"He said you were supposed to talk tonight, but he was falling asleep on the couch, so I told him to just go to bed and that you two could talk in the morning." He glanced at the guest room door and then back at me.

"Yeah. Tomorrow morning is good." I walked over to the tin and grabbed a couple of squares of shortbread and flopped into the chair across from him. The truth was, I wasn't in any shape to talk to Kennedy at that moment anyway. It was better for both of us if I had time to process everything that had happened that day.

"No luck on the finding spell?" Jax asked.

I leaned my head back and closed my eyes, willing myself to find the energy to explain everything that happened in the last few hours. When I opened them again, Jax was staring at me, concern radiating from his expression.

"Marion? What happened?"

I took a deep breath, explained how the coven hadn't shown up, about the man who attacked Hollister, and then the message he delivered.

By the time I was finished recanting the encounter with the mysterious stranger, Jax was pacing and visibly upset.

"Jax?" I asked. "Are you all right?"

He stopped suddenly and stared right at me. "Am I all right?

Am I? No. I'm not. The woman I've loved for most of my life was threatened by someone who could've killed Hollister, and I'm finding out about it hours later. Hell, I've just been sitting here eating cookies when I could've been doing something, anything, to keep you safe."

"Hey," I said, blowing out a long breath. "There was nothing you could do. If you'd been there, it's likely you would've suffered the same fate as Hollister."

"That's not the point, Marion," he said, walking over to me and kneeling in front of me. "You've been doing everything you can to help your friend, putting yourself in the line of fire. Meanwhile, I'm dealing with insurance claims, investigations with the Magical Task Force, and eating cookies instead of helping you. From now on, I want to be with you when you go looking for Kiera. It's just too dangerous."

I appreciated that he didn't automatically jump to the conclusion that I'd stop looking for Kiera just because I'd had a run-in with someone who'd threatened me. Jax knew me. He understood that I'd never be able to live with myself if I didn't help a friend who needed me. But he didn't know everything. Not yet. I reached out and took his hand while sliding over to share my oversized chair with him.

He slid in next to me and put his arm around me, holding me close.

"There's more," I said.

Jax stiffened and then swept his gaze over me as if inspecting every square inch of my body. "Tell me that man didn't hurt you."

"He didn't," I said, leaning into him, grateful to be wrapped in his arms. It was easier to tell him the hard stuff when we were touching. Somehow I just felt like as long as he was here,

we'd get through anything. Even the guilt of giving up on a
friend who may or may not have been lying to me for years.

"What happened? Did he coerce you? Threaten you? Rob
you?" Jax was practically vibrating with tension.

Ignoring the slight twinge still aching in my shoulder, I
placed my hand on his chest and looked up to meet his gaze.
"None of that. I already told you everything that went on at the
coven circle. This is about what I learned at Gigi and
Sebastian's afterward."

THE TENSION slowly drained from his body as he let out a long
sigh of relief. But when he shifted slightly, and I winced, he bit
off a curse. "You're still hurt. Let me get you some pain killers,
and then you can give me the rest of the story."

I sat in the chair, watching as he disappeared into my
kitchen. It wasn't long before he emerged with a glass of water
and a couple of pills.

He handed them to me, and after I downed them, he tugged
me out of the chair and led me over to the couch. "This should
be a little more comfortable."

"What did I ever do without you?" I asked, taking up
position in the corner of the sofa.

"I'm sure you managed just fine." He took a seat and turned
toward me. "You've always been an independently strong
woman." Jax let out a sardonic chuckle. "You still very much are,
and I wouldn't have it any other way. But I do hope you'll let me
take care of you when the situation arises, because if there is
one thing you deserve, Marion Matched, it's for someone to
care for you the way you care for everyone else in your life."

Dammit. Those tears were stinging the backs of my eyes

again. I blinked them back, determined to not break down. Crying in front of him wasn't an issue. I wasn't afraid to show vulnerability. Not usually. But if I started crying now, I wasn't sure I'd stop. Every last one of my nerves was on edge.

Jax pressed a palm to my cheek. "You're okay, Marion. It's just you and me right now."

I gave him a small smile. He was so sweet and kind and everything I never realized I'd needed. For so long, I'd focused on the passion between us, but I'd forgotten that Jax could really see me. He saw right through my bravado and the tough-businesswoman persona I wore like armor and really saw the woman beneath it all, the one who cared so deeply it sometimes hurt. "Thanks. You're right. I'm okay. Or I will be, because the search is over."

He frowned, confusion painting his features. "You found her?"

I shook my head slowly. "No. Sebastian found out that she's a former Magical Task Force agent and ran when she was indicted for manslaughter. And Iris got a visit from a friend in the Magical Task Force who warned her that if we kept looking, we could be in legal jeopardy if we helped her in any way."

Jax's eyes widened with surprise, but he quickly narrowed them as he started putting two and two together. "That's a very good reason for not wanting someone to call law enforcement if she goes MIA."

"Yes. It is." I'd had that thought more than once, but there was still doubt nagging at me. And for good reason. "The only thing I can't reconcile is why she told Garrison to come to me if she went missing. That implies she wanted to be found, right? I don't get it."

He shrugged. "Maybe she never wanted Garrison to know her real past and figured you'd tell him her cover story."

"Maybe," I said with a shrug. Jax's theory was a little bit of a stretch, but it made a certain amount of sense, I supposed. Still, that didn't stop me from doubting my decision to stop searching when that tingle at the base of my spine appeared again.

"Is the consensus that she's been picked up by the agency then?" Jax asked.

"Maybe. But either way, with the warning at the coven circle, and then learning about the charges against her, it seems clear it's far too dangerous to keep searching," I said, feeling cold inside. "I hate giving up on looking for her. The Kiera I knew was kind and a salt-of-the-earth type person. My heart says that if she did kill someone, it was either a tragedy or there was a really good reason. My head says that there are always multiple sides to people and just because I knew one version of her, that doesn't mean another one doesn't exist. And I just can't risk putting everyone I love in danger. Not Ty, Kennedy, my dad, Lucy... you."

Jax didn't say anything else. He just pulled me into his arms and held me. As I pressed my cheek to his chest, I finally gave in to the overwhelming emotion that I'd been tamping down ever since Sebastian had delivered the unsettling news. The tears started to fall, and I cried for the friend I knew and prayed I hadn't made the wrong decision. That she wasn't being held by an abusive ex while we all moved on with our lives as if she'd never existed.

Because if there was one thing I knew for sure, it was that if I found out Kiera had been telling the truth the entire time, I'd never forgive myself for giving up on her.

CHAPTER 16

"Coffee," I muttered as I dragged myself into the kitchen the next morning.

"Already made," Kennedy said.

I jumped slightly, startled by the sound of his voice. "Good goddess," I said, placing my hand over my heart as I spotted Kennedy at the table with a mug and a plate with a half-eaten piece of toast in front of him. "You scared the bejesus out of me. I didn't see you there."

"Sorry about that." He gave me a shaky smile. "I thought you were talking to me."

I gave him a sheepish smile. "I was just muttering to myself."

Kennedy rose from the chair and promptly started fixing my coffee, complete with my favorite creamer.

"You don't need to do that," I said, heading to the fridge to rummage up something to eat.

"I've already got breakfast started," he said, handing me the mug. "Sit and enjoy your coffee while I finish up."

I glanced at the stove, noting there was a pan sitting there and a package of bacon next to it. The oven was on, and now that I was paying attention, the faint scent of fresh biscuits was starting to fill the air. "You were sent from heaven, weren't you?"

He chuckled and waved me over to the table.

"Seriously, if I'd known you could cook, I might have just hired you as my fulltime chef," I said.

"Stop. I used to work at a small mom and pop diner in high school. On the weekends I sometimes filled in for the owner." He got busy with the bacon and then scrambled some eggs. By the time he was done, I was practically drooling.

"Goat-cheese eggs, hickory smoked bacon, and fresh biscuits," he said, placing a plate in front of me. "I'd have made gravy, but you didn't have any sausage. I'll do that next time."

"Gravy? You make homemade sausage gravy?" I stared at him wide-eyed. "Seriously. You were sent by the gods, right? I'm not sure I deserve this."

"You deserve a lot more than a greasy spoon-style breakfast," Kennedy said, taking a seat next to me. "Trust me on that one."

I took a bite of the goat-cheese eggs and nearly died of happiness. "These are delicious. Seriously, if you like to cook, just make me a list and I'll be sure to stock the fridge with whatever you need."

His face lit up with a genuine smile that made my heart soar. "I do like to cook. But I'll get the groceries. Skyler told me yesterday that if I prove to be trustworthy, he'll consider hiring me as a paid intern after I'm done working off my payment for the trouble yesterday."

"He did?" I put my fork down and gave Kennedy my full attention. "Are you interested in fashion design?"

Kennedy's face flushed light pink as he nodded. "I could be. Skyler's an interesting person."

I raised one eyebrow, studying him. "You know Skyler is married, right?"

Kennedy jerked his head slightly and then blinked at me. "What?"

"He has a husband. They live next to Gigi."

"Right," he stuttered out. "Yes, I did know that." His flush deepened. "I didn't mean to imply I was interested in Skyler. I mean, he's old enough to be my dad."

I chuckled. "Oh, the horror. I thought daddies were a thing in gay culture."

"Oh. My. God. Stop it, Marion," he said, sputtering with laughter.

"Okay, I'll stop." I grinned, enjoying our easy interaction. "Tell me about this internship. How did that happen?"

He shrugged one shoulder as if to say it was no big deal, but he couldn't hide the tiny smile tugging at his lips.

"Come on. Tell Mama Marion the deets," I coaxed.

He threw his head back and laughed. "Deets?"

"Details. Come on. Spill."

"Oh, I don't speak boomer. Sorry," he teased.

I scoffed. "I'm Gen-X, thank you very much."

"My apologies," he said with a snicker, but then he sobered. "Yesterday after I finished checking in all the inventory, I helped Skyler price everything. While we were working, he told me a little bit about his family, which led to me talking about mine." Kennedy frowned and pinched his brows together as he added, "We have a lot in common."

I nodded. "He said something about having a difficult family earlier."

Kennedy nodded. "It's more than that, though. His family

didn't accept him either when he came out, so there's that. But that's not all that uncommon, you know."

My jaw tensed. As long as I lived, I'd never understand anyone casting their child aside just because of who they loved. That made no sense to me whatsoever. "Yeah. Unfortunately."

"It turns out we had a lot of the same interests. Theater, ice skating, hanging out at the library. You know, decidedly uncool things for shy, skinny boys in high school."

That made me angry, too. "You know, for a country so hung up on celebrity culture, I'll never understand why the drama kids are uncool. Those are the ones who are going to grow up to be famous. Like the kids in band. Where exactly do people think musicians get their start?"

"That leaves out ice skating and book lovers. I guess nerds deserve their reputation for those things." He winked and took a long sip of coffee.

"Please. Authors are cool," I said.

"They are only rock stars to book nerds," Kennedy insisted.

I grudgingly agreed. "Still, those interests are far more fascinating than people seem to realize when they're teenagers."

He snorted. "You can say that again."

"So, you two have stuff in common. Sounds like you bonded some."

Kennedy nodded. "We did. He also told me that he had a rough time after he cut off contact with his family and it took him a while to trust people again." His voice trailed off as he pushed the food around his plate. "He asked if maybe that's why I left here when I didn't have to."

I put my fork down, making sure Kennedy had my full attention. "What did you say?"

"Nothing at first," he admitted. "But then... I said, maybe?"

He met my gaze. "I think he was onto something. I have real trust issues, but I want you to know it's not you. I do trust you. I'm just having trouble trusting my own judgment."

I reached over and placed my hand over his. "When the people you trust the most turn their back on you, it's completely normal to start questioning everything you've ever believed. Do you think that's also why you're distancing yourself from Ty?"

"Yes. No." He quickly shook his head. "I mean, I'm sure that's part of it, but the main problem is that I'm too afraid that I'll start to lean on him too much. He's so independent and has direction. He's out there living his dream, and I'm... flailing. What am I doing except clinging to a man who isn't even here?"

"It's okay to take some time to figure out what you're going to do with your life. Especially when the rug has been pulled out from under you," I said gently. "What were you doing down in LA before you came up here."

He let out a sardonic laugh. "Assisting my mother with her landscape design business."

"Oh, ouch." Not only had he lost his family, he'd lost his job, too.

"Yeah. Ouch. I lost everything and just followed Ty here. Then he left, and suddenly, I had no idea what I was doing or why I was here." He let out a long sigh. "I have a degree in business management and no idea what I want to be doing for a job. That's pathetic."

"No it isn't," I assured him. "It's normal. So many people get college degrees then end up not going into that field. The important thing is that you have one, so any job you decide on, you won't hit a glass ceiling because you don't have that piece of paper on the wall."

"I guess. It all just seemed so meaningless there for a while. I thought that if I left, I'd be forced to figure myself out. Instead, I found myself mixed up with someone who had no problem spelling me without my consent and then left me to take the fall for his crime. My decision-making has been less than desirable. But staying here and working with Skyler just feels right in a way that nothing else has… except for when I'm with Ty."

A weight seemed to lift off my shoulders as his words sank in. He was finding his way, and I just knew that if he managed to stay out of trouble, Skyler would be an excellent mentor. If designing clothes turned out to be his thing, I knew Skyler would help him in every way he knew how. Skyler was just that sort of person.

"Try to pay attention to that inner voice," I said. "I've found that when I listen to what my intuition is telling me, that's when I'm making my best decisions."

He nodded. "I'm going to try."

"Good, because I like having you here, but if you break the rules, I won't hesitate to show you the door."

Kennedy's face turned white as he nervously licked his bottom lip. "Okay. What are the rules?"

I gave him an easy smile. "Two things. Stay out of trouble and don't forget to check in if you're not going to come home. I'm a worrier."

"That's it?" he asked, looking skeptical. "Aren't there any chores or a deadline to pay rent or move out? How about visitors? Are they allowed, or would you prefer that I meet up with friends elsewhere?"

"That's it. The only chores I expect you to do are to clean up after yourself. There's no rent or move out date. I'm happy to have you here as long as you like. As for friends, they are welcome as long as they aren't rowdy. If one happens to be a boyfriend type, I only ask that you and Ty figure your relationship out first before you bring anyone else around."

Kennedy stared at me, seeming incredulous. Then he shook his head. "I'll cook when I can, which means I'll clean up as I go. I'll clean the second bathroom at least once a week. And as far as boyfriends, the only person I'm interested in seeing is my actual boyfriend, Ty. You don't have to worry about that. I might be messed up, but I'm faithful. But I may invite a few friends over for a *Housewives* marathon. Care to join us?"

"A *Housewives* marathon?" I asked, amused. "That depends. Are there margaritas involved?"

His eyes twinkled with mischief as he nodded. "Always."

CHAPTER 17

"*K*nock, knock!" Aunt Lucy's voice was followed by the sound of my front door swinging open. "You're lucky I'm decent," I called from the kitchen, where I was busy finishing the breakfast dishes.

"Ha!" she said as she appeared in the kitchen doorway. "I was hoping Jax was still here and I'd get a glimpse of some man candy, but it looks like I'll just have to go back to *Abs, Buns, and Guns* for an oiled-up, hot-man gun show."

I sputtered with laughter. "Did you think Jax was going to be walking around in his boxer briefs and lubed up with baby oil?"

"Of course not. But after eating all the shortbread, it was possible he'd have butter glistening from his pores."

Still chuckling, I held my arms open and invited her in for a hug.

My aunt wrapped her arms around me and squeezed me tightly. "It feels like I haven't seen you in ages."

"It's been less than a week," I said as I pulled back. "But

you're right. It feels like longer. Thank you for the cookies by the way. They were exactly what I needed last night."

She pressed her hand to my cheek and smiled. "You're welcome, my dear. You know how much I enjoy fattening up the people I love."

I pressed my hand to my stomach and nodded. "You're definitely succeeding. I'm gonna have to clear everything off my treadmill and get my butt moving if I plan to fit into my favorite jeans again."

"*Pfft.* Cookies are far superior to any jeans," she insisted. "Keep the cookies. Sell the treadmill."

"Easy for you to say." I eyed her trim figure. "You seem to have the metabolism of a twenty-year-old."

She tucked a lock of her ash blond hair behind one ear and gave me a sly smile. "There's more than one way to exercise."

I raised one eyebrow. "What exactly are you trying to say? Did you find someone here in Premonition Pointe to... uh... date?" The visual of my aunt doing the horizontal mambo flashed in my mind, and I suddenly wanted to dunk my head into a bath of soapy water. That wasn't an image I needed in my head. But if she had found someone to spice up her sex life, then good for her. She deserved to have some fun.

"I wouldn't exactly call it dating," she said, flushing. "More like..." She frowned. "What do you kids call it? A booty call?"

"Did you really just say booty call?" My lips twitched with amusement.

"Yes. Was that not the right term? Fine. We Netflix and chill a few times a week."

"Stop!" I cried, holding my hand out. "This isn't something you should be telling your niece."

"Oh, please, Marion," she scoffed. "You're a matchmaker. Surely you've heard worse."

"Of course I have, but not from my favorite aunt. As happy as I am for you, sometimes certain things should be left unsaid."

She rolled her eyes and sat down at the table. "Forget about my Tinder date. I'm here about something much more serious."

Thankful we were past the Tinder portion of the conversation, I held up the coffee pot in question.

"Yes." She gave me a decisive nod. "And if there are any cookies left, we're going to need those, too."

"Of course." I fixed us both coffee and put the tin of cookies on the table as I took a seat next to her.

"Jax sure did some damage to these." She picked up one cookie and nibbled on the corner before taking a long sip of the coffee. Her eyes closed as she savored the drink, and when she opened them, she said, "This is the absolute best way to start the day."

I almost countered that the only way it was better was if someone made you breakfast, but I kept the thought to myself because knowing Lucy, she was more interested in the company than the coffee or the cookies.

There was a sudden pop and Celia appeared in the chair directly across from my aunt. "I prefer a couple of orgasms, but to each her own."

"Celia! That's my aunt," I cried.

"So?" Celia pushed her long blond hair over her shoulder and smirked at me. "I'm sure she knows what an orgasm is."

"You know it, girlfriend," Aunt Lucy said, pumping her eyebrows. "I have got to tell you about that one night back in the late eighties when I went out with a Brad Pitt look-a-like and when he went down—"

"Is there a reason we've been blessed with your company?" I

asked the ghost dryly, cutting off my aunt. I just didn't need those kinds of details. "Or are you just here for a visit?"

"Mostly just a visit. Wanted to let you know Kennedy and Skyler are getting along nicely. It's rather boring watching him now. All he does is follow Skyler around and ask him all kinds of questions about designing clothes and running that store."

Kennedy had left for Sky's the Limit not long after we'd finished breakfast. And although it'd been clear that Kennedy was grateful to be working for Skyler, it was nice to get the confirmation from Celia that he really was interested in learning. "That's good news. Looks like you're free to do whatever you'd like for a while."

Celia pursed her lips. "What? You don't have anything else for me to oversee? What about your friend who is missing?"

I frowned. It hadn't occurred to me to keep Celia on the case. Though the idea was brilliant. She could be on the lookout while also keeping a low profile. It would be a way to keep looking for Kiera without putting everyone I knew in danger. "Celia, you're brilliant."

"Well, duh. That's what I have been telling you. It's about time you caught up." She gave me a hair flip befitting a shampoo commercial.

Chuckling, I shook my head. "You're right. I should've listened to you sooner. Here's what's going on with Kiera's case." I quickly filled her in on all the details, including the fact that the Magical Task Force had warned us to not interfere.

"She killed someone?" Celia narrowed her eyes. "Do we know why?"

I shook my head. "We don't have any details."

"I bet whoever she offed was a real dick and deserved it," Celia said. "You know I love men. Love them. But some of them, they can be total trash. It would not surprise me one bit if she did us all a favor and took out the garbage."

"Celia," Aunt Lucy tsked. "That's quite a leap, don't you think? Marion just told us we don't have any details. We don't know the circumstances. Anything could have happened. It's probably not a good idea to jump to conclusions."

Celia shrugged. "Just a theory. But I'll be happy to look for her. Where do I start?"

"I have no idea," I said. "Perhaps hang around with the Magical Task Force? See if you can get any intel?"

"Where do I find them?" she asked.

"An agent is investigating the explosion at Jax's construction site. Start with him. Follow him around."

"Oooooh. Yesssss." Celia rubbed her hands together as her big eyes twinkled with mischief. "I like this plan. I always wanted to know what those agents did day in and day out. It seems like most of them just take notes and write reports. But maybe I'll get to see some serious magical showdowns."

"Just make sure you stay under the radar," I said sternly. Celia had a habit of popping in and running her mouth when she was bored or annoyed or just wanted attention. "If they find out you're associated with me and are spilling their secrets, that could mean serious trouble. Understand?"

The ghost rolled her eyes. "I'm not an idiot, Marion. I can stay invisible while stalking the agents."

I bit my lower lip, wondering if this was a mistake. "They *are* Magical Task Force agents," I said again. "It's possible they have ghost detectors of some sort. You're going to need to be careful that you aren't detected."

"I'll just say I'm there to keep an eye on Jax," she said flippantly. "Or that I have a crush on one of the construction workers. You don't need to worry about me. I'm a crafty ghost." She winked and then disappeared into thin air again.

"She's colorful," my aunt said.

"She is," I agreed and then grimaced. "Did I just make a mistake asking her to do that?"

Aunt Lucy covered my hand with hers. "You're doing what you need to do. I heard everything you said about the Magical Task Force and what happened at the coven circle. The truth is, no one really knows the real story. And you've known her longer than anybody. You have to go with your gut. It's obvious to me you're not completely convinced that she's *not* the victim here. Sending Celia is a sensible solution for the time being. As long as she's discreet, this is a good compromise."

"Discretion isn't exactly her strong suit," I said.

"I know," she said with a nod. "But I have confidence she can handle it."

"You're probably right," I said, even though I wasn't so sure. But what could I do about it now? Nothing. I just had to say a prayer to the goddesses that sending Celia wasn't a complete fuckup. "Now, tell me why you're visiting," I said, turning my attention to my aunt. "Something tells me it's not just to sit and eat the cookies you delivered yesterday."

"Maybe I just wanted to see my niece," she said.

I snorted. "Sure. I'll buy that when you stop nervously crumbling that cookie."

Lucy looked down at the crumbs piled in front of her and let out a curse. "Fine. You got me. I'm here because of your father."

"Dad?" My blood pressure spiked and I had to fight the urge to jump to my feet. Obviously, I was still on edge after the events of the past couple of weeks. "What's wrong?"

"He's messing up his life. That's what's wrong," she huffed out. "I'm telling you, that man is going to be alone for the rest of his life if he doesn't get his act together."

I blinked at her. "You're talking about him and Tazia?"

"Of course I am. Who else?" She stood abruptly and started to pace the kitchen. "He's been on three dates with three different women in the past week. None of them Tazia. And when I asked him what he was doing, he brushed me off and told me to mind my own business."

"That's… disappointing," I muttered. Dad had been a dating nightmare ever since my mom left him decades ago. But Tazia was his perfect match, and they really liked each other. I'd thought that he'd finally turned a corner and was going to give their relationship a chance. "Did something happened between them, or is this just Dad being Dad?"

"It's just your father being himself. You know how he is, and if he keeps it up, he's going to completely ruin his chances with Tazia. I swear, he makes me want to scream at him sometimes. Tazia is lovely. If I had to choose, I'd take her over my thick-headed brother."

"No you wouldn't," I said mildly. "But I share your frustration. I'm just not sure what I can do about it. I can't force him to date her. I wouldn't even if I could. It has to be his choice."

"I know." Lucy stopped her pacing and placed both palms on the counter as she stared me in the eye. "But that doesn't mean we can't do something to light a fire under his ass."

My lips twitched with amusement. "What are you proposing exactly?"

"Set Tazia up with a few men. Let him get a taste of his own medicine. You heard that she saw him on that date the other morning, right?" Lucy sounded disgusted.

"Yeah," I said with a sigh. "But I can't do that unless Tazia asks me to."

"Oh, she's open to it. Trust me."

I eyed her. "You talked to Tazia about this?"

Lucy nodded decisively and then pulled out her phone. She put it on speaker and dialed Tazia's number.

"Hey, Lucy. What's up?" Tazia asked when she answered.

"I'm just confirming that you'd like to see about dating someone other than my brother."

"Um, well…" Tazia's voice trailed off.

"I have Marion here and she says she doesn't want to play matchmaker unless you really want her to. What do you say? Do you want to show my brother exactly what he's missing by dating half the town?"

Silence.

"Lucy," I said gently. "We don't need to put Tazia on the spot like this. Tazia, if you want to give dating a shot, just give me a call or come by the office. I can always set up a mixer or let you go through some profiles and see if we find a match."

"No!" Tazia said suddenly.

"Okay, that's fine, too. No one is trying to pressure you," I said.

"No, I mean I don't need to think about it. Go ahead and plan a mixer. I'll be there." The conviction in her tone was clear. The woman who was perfect for my father was done playing his game.

"Well then… good for you," I said, smiling. Maybe this really would be a wake-up call for my commitment-phobe father. I knew he liked Tazia. He just couldn't bring himself to let go of the past and let himself be happy. "I'm planning a mixer this week for a new client. He's in your age range. How about you join us? I'll be sure to invite a handful of other hopefuls, and we can go from there."

"Just tell me when and where. I'll be there," she said.

"That's my girl," Lucy said, looking pleased with herself.

Tazia chuckled and said her goodbyes.

Once the call ended, I turned to my aunt. "I hope you're prepared for the possibility that she might actually find someone she wants to date who isn't Dad."

"Oh, I'm prepared. I just don't think Memphis is," she said with a gleam in her eyes. "And it'll serve him right."

"Poor Dad," I said. "How's he going to survive Premonition Pointe with the two of us ganging up on him?"

"He'll either sink or swim." Lucy pressed a kiss to the top of my head, grabbed another couple of cookies and waved as she headed for the front door. "I'll talk to you later. Gotta go shopping for a new outfit for the mixer."

"You're coming?" I asked, following her.

"Sure. I wouldn't miss this for the world."

As the door slammed behind her, I made a note to invite a few men her age. If she was going to meddle in Dad's love life, turnabout was fair play.

CHAPTER 18

"*J*'m telling you, Marion," Tandy said. "This is a giant clusterfuck. I've never seen a production go off the rails like this before."

I glanced at the phone I'd clipped into a holder and eyed my friend over Facetime. "It can't be that bad, can it? The show has barely started production."

I was in the office, working on the final details for the night's mixer for Brix Belford. It had been four days since I'd stopped looking for Kiera, and I'd thrown all my effort into the mixer, mostly just to keep my mind occupied. Celia was still keeping an eye on the Magical Task Force agent, but she'd said it was about as exciting as watching her nana pluck her mustache.

"It *is* that bad," Tandy said with an exaggerated eye roll. "The director decided to rewrite the script, and now it's a misogynistic disaster with a dude-bro hero and a heroine who has less brain cells than a sex bot."

"That is bad," I agreed. "Lennon must love that." Lennon Love, a popular social media influencer, was the star of Tandy's new project, and the very idea that she'd play a one-dimensional character was unthinkable. The woman was smart and dynamic. No way would she fade into a role. Not to mention her fans would revolt. The show would be over before it even started.

"She's threatening to back out." Tandy made a frustrated face. "Can't say I'd blame her if this was the final scrip. Thank the goddess I have final say over everything. This is being thrown out, along with the director, and I'll be re-writing. It's just going to take a bit of time. Time I was supposed to take off and spend with you."

"Who is this director?" I asked, annoyed for both of us. It wasn't like I got to spend much time with my bestie. She was an in-demand show runner for a the most popular paranormal network in Hollywood. Her trip being cut short because of a jackass director sucked rough broomsticks.

"Some guy my executive producer hired after the last one fell and broke his leg and had to pull out of the project. I swear on everything magical, these jackasses need to keep their grubby hands off my productions, or I'm going to find a way to take my shows elsewhere."

"Don't say that too loudly. You know how cagey they get." If they knew she was trying to leave for another network, they'd do everything in their power to take her projects away from her.

Her eyes were narrowed and her expression was fierce when she said, "Just let them try."

"I wouldn't go up against you." I grinned at her.

"*You* would never have to." Tandy winked and then sobered. "Okay, onto something more important."

I raised both eyebrows. "There's something more important than your project imploding?"

"It's Ty."

I froze and gave her my full attention. "What's going on with Ty? I just texted with him yesterday. He didn't say anything. What happened?"

"He's miserable," she said without preamble.

"Why?"

"He hates his job but is so proud and determined to get ahead that he won't walk."

"Okay, you're gonna have to explain," I said. "He told me it's great there. That he'd already been offered a job after this one ends. What do you know that I don't?"

"The producer he's working for is a jackass. It sounds like he's done a one-eighty since Ty was hired. Now he's making Ty work late every night and is having him redo the sound on scenes that are already excellent. I don't get it. I've heard good things about his boss, but just this past week, it's turned into a nightmare scenario. I told Ty he should walk. No one should be working under those conditions, but he won't do it. He doesn't want a reputation of quitting before a job is done."

"I can understand that," I said. "But I hate that this is happening. Hollywood isn't the only place a sound guy can get work."

"I said the same thing." She sighed. "This business is the shits sometimes. Maybe I shouldn't have said anything, but I thought you should know what's going on. If he's distant or seems exhausted, that's why."

"Thanks, Tandy. I do appreciate it, even if I feel like there's nothing I can do."

My friend gave me a sympathetic smile. "Maybe just check in on him so he knows you have his back. I also think he's pretty upset about Kennedy, but he won't talk about it."

"Yeah. I bet."

"Listen, Mar, I've got to go. Take care of yourself. I'll call when I can." Tandy ended the call, leaving me with a blank phone.

My fingers itched to call Ty immediately, but he never picked up during the day when he was working. I'd be better off calling after dinner. Except it would have to be later than that. I had the mixer to attend, and if things went well, I'd make sure at least three people were matched.

The door swung open, and Iris walked in. "I'm here! Sorry I'm late. I was busy talking to Hope about the mixer tonight."

Hope Anderson was putting the mixer together for us. After the last one I'd hosted ended with a fire from the candles I'd picked out, I'd decided to leave the details to a professional party planner.

"No need to apologize. You were taking care of business," I said, swinging my chair around to greet her.

"I was," she said, nodding in agreement. "I just forgot to let you know."

"It's fine. Really." I flipped open the file on my desk and started scanning the names of the people on the guest list. "I figured you were busy with last-minute details."

She gave me a grateful smile and then eyed the folder. "Did you get enough matches for Brix?"

I groaned. "I only have two good prospects, and one of them is Tazia. Can you believe that?"

"You're going to fix him up with your dad's girlfriend?" Iris asked, sounding incredulous.

"She's not my dad's girlfriend. In fact, I think they've only been out once." The words left a bad taste in my mouth. Why did my dad have to be so resistant to falling in love again? I knew the answer, I just didn't want to accept it.

"That's too bad," Iris said. "They seem perfect for each other."

"They are," Celia said, popping into existence. She sat on the edge of my desk and let out a very put-upon sigh. "Do you have any idea how boring Mr. By The Book really is?"

"I assume you mean Agent Erikson?" I asked.

"Gods, yes. All the man does is read files and bark at his secretary." She flopped her ghostly body down on the desk and flung her arms to the side as if she were completely giving up. "He doesn't even go out. All he does is go to the office, read his files, and then get take out before he goes home. Then he watches two hours of the History Channel. I swear, if I were still alive, I think my eyes would be bleeding by now."

"Why would your eyes be bleeding?" Iris asked curiously.

"Because I would have stabbed them by now." She sat up and her eyes pleaded with me. "Do I really have to keep tagging along with him?"

"Not if he isn't leading you to any clues. But have you taken a look at his files?"

She groaned. "I tried, but his handwriting is awful. Besides, the files are about Jax's site, and it sounds like they've hit a dead end there."

"If it's a dead end, then why is he studying the files all the time?" I asked.

"How am I supposed to know?" she asked dramatically. "Maybe he's just trying to stay busy so he doesn't have to work on the other case that just came in."

"What new case?" Iris asked.

"I don't know. Something about illegal spells being created in some shop down in LA. Sounds like normal Magical Task Force kind of stuff. They are putting together a team to go investigate." She waved a dismissive hand. "I don't think it has anything to do with Kiera or the explosion here."

"Probably not," I said. My plan to have Celia spy on the task force agents was turning out to be a bust. "You haven't heard anything interesting at all?"

"Hmm, I didn't say that." She snickered. "It turns out the main boss is sleeping with at least two of the agents... at the same time. It's the only thing any of them can talk about. You'd think none of them had ever had a threesome before."

"No wonder no one ever talks about the cases," I muttered.

"Why would they when they're all trying to figure out which one she's going to tie up later? I'm telling you, it's a full-on soap opera up in that joint." Celia shook her head in disgust. "Even *I'm* tired of it. Is that *all* they ever think about?"

I met Iris's gaze and we both started laughing. Iris laughed so hard her eyes started to water.

"Yeah, okay. I realize that sounds ridiculous coming from me, but seriously. They're a law enforcement agency." She threw her hands up in defeat. "It's just unprofessional."

"She has a point," Iris said, gasping for breath.

"She does," I agreed and then frowned. If the agency was so unprofessional that the boss was sleeping with two of her subordinates, could we really trust what they'd said about Kiera? Just from the little that Celia had told us about the office, I wasn't inclined to trust anything they said. "Celia?"

"Yes?" the ghost said, sounding put out.

"What's your assessment of the agents? Besides the ones sleeping with the boss, do you think they are the type to follow the rules or do they seem—"

"Corrupt?" she finished for me.

"Yeah. Corrupt is a good word."

She pursed her lips together and then gave me a

noncommittal shrug. "Maybe? None of them seem married to the job."

"What do you mean by that?" Iris asked, coming to stand next to me. "That they don't care? Maybe are sloppy about investigating?"

"No. It's not that," Celia said. "I'd say it's more that they just don't have a sense of urgency. Like yesterday, a call came in about a potential curse that was affecting all the men at a retirement village, and they all just laughed and took their time playing rock paper scissors to see who was going to deal with it."

"All the men were cursed? How?" I asked.

"Oh, that." She rolled her eyes. "It turns out one of the witches cursed their penis pills, and instead of erections they ended up with incontinence. They were peeing in the pool so much it was starting to turn green."

"That's... not cool," I said, grimacing at the thought of how much urine it would take to turn a pool green.

"Neither is poking a woman with your penis pill boner," Celia said. "Which is supposedly what started the entire thing when a group of five of them had too much cider and decided to use their boners to flirt with the ladies. Consent is a real issue with that crowd."

"I'd say so," Iris said, sounding disgusted. I had to admit she had a point.

"Anyway," Celia continued, "I'd have thought the agents would've loved to handle that problem. That was A-plus drama right there. Right up their alley."

"It doesn't sound like anything is up their alley. That doesn't instill confidence that they are really working on Jax's case or that they told us the truth about Kiera."

Iris bit down on her bottom lip before nodding. "You know,

as much as I hate to admit it, I think you're right."

I turned to Celia. "Do you think you could get us some records?"

The ghost held up her hands and then plunged them right through my computer. "See that? I can't make contact with anything other than another ghost. So no. But I could get you into the office after hours so you can get the files yourself."

I was half a second away from agreeing when Iris shook her head. "No. Absolutely not. Do you know what they'd do to us if they found us snooping around the offices? I don't even think we'd get a trial. They'd just throw us in a cell and call it a day. The Magical Task Force doesn't mess around. Stolen files are a huge-ass deal to them. Like top-secret type stuff."

They did monitor and regulate the use of magic. It made sense there'd be harsh punishments for anyone stealing information, especially if that information was illicit spells and curses. "Yeah, Iris is right. We can't do that. I wish we could, but it's too risky. Maybe for now you should just go back and take a look around at the files and eavesdrop on who's working late. Maybe you'll hear something."

She groaned. "It's so boring there. I want to go to the mixer tonight. The last one was such a blast."

"Of fire," I muttered, but then I gave her a cheerful smile. "How about you go snoop around for a while, and then you can join us at the mixer later. I'll save you a champagne glass."

Celia rolled her eyes at my champagne comment but didn't acknowledge it further. "Fine. But I'll be there at eight o'clock sharp." She started to fade away but before she disappeared completely, I heard her add, "Or seven if I get too bored."

The loud pop sounded, indicating that she was gone. Iris and I stared at each other for a moment before we both started chattering at once.

"Who's in charge of that task force?" Iris asked.

"Who's poking women with their boners?"

Iris shook her head at me, giving me a half smile while managing a you-can't-be-serious look. My face heated when I realized I'd narrowed in on the least important information that Celia had given us. I cleared my throat. "Um, I mean, we should really find out more about the agent in charge and determine if she runs her department as negligently as Celia thinks or if our ghost is just exaggerating."

Iris chuckled. She grabbed her phone and dialed. It wasn't long before she said, "Agent Stevens, I need a favor."

CHAPTER 19

"*A*ny idea when Agent Stevens will get back to you?" I asked Iris as we walked over to the open bar. We'd finished checking in the guests twenty minutes ago and were giving Brix and his hopefuls a chance to get to know each other. We were on the heated patio at Hallucinations, a beachside bar that sold cocktails with names like Lost Your Bikini and Surfer's Tan. But since we'd rented the space, we were serving wine, martinis, and champagne and had appetizers for the guests.

"A few days at least." Iris ordered a martini with two olives, making me raise one eyebrow. She rarely drank anything other than a half glass of champagne at these events. "It's been a strange day," she said as she leaned against the bar, watching the guests mill about. "Stevens was pretty taken aback by the sexual allegations. She said if it was remotely true, careers were going to be ruined."

"I would imagine so." The bartender handed me a glass of red wine, and I spotted Tazia walking over to Brix to introduce herself. She looked fabulous in her turquoise and brown boho dress with its oversized sleeves and knee-high, brown suede lace-up boots. Her auburn hair flowed in waves down her back. There wasn't a day that she didn't rock that flower-child hippy look, but tonight, she just looked retro-glamorous.

"They look good together," Iris said.

"No argument here." Brix was wearing an expensive bright blue suit with a white button-down shirt that was open at the collar, giving him a sexy vibe that was completed by his five o'clock shadow. He was about ten years younger than Tazia, but neither of them seemed to care, considering she had her hand on his arm while he had one hand on her hip. The two of them were laughing and obviously enjoying each other's company.

"There's Memphis," Iris said.

I followed her gaze across the patio and spotted my father scowling as he watched Tazia and Brix.

"He doesn't look all that pleased," she said.

"Serves him right," I said with a soft chuckle. Maybe Aunt Lucy had been right. It certainly appeared that seeing Tazia enjoying her time with another man might just be the kick in the pants my father needed.

I glanced at the entrance to the adjoining restaurant. Jax had texted that he was going to meet me here after he ran home and showered. Between the time I'd spent looking for Kiera and his extra time at the work site, we just hadn't seen much of each other. He hadn't even come over the past two nights because he'd been working so much overtime and trying to get the project back on schedule.

"Who are you waiting on?" Iris asked, following my gaze.

"My date," I said, smiling at her. "You know you don't have to stay, right? All the guests are here. Hope's already been here and gone. She made sure everything was just right before she was called away to deal with another event that was also scheduled tonight. The mixer appears to be going smoothly. The only thing left to do is talk to Brix at the end of the evening to find out who he's most interested in dating. Then a little cleanup and we'll be good to go."

"I know," she said. "But sometimes it's just nice to be out, enjoying a cocktail." She held her martini up. "This is delicious. Besides, Kade is out with Lucas having a beer. The only one waiting for me at home is Bunny. She won't mind if I stay out a little longer."

I chuckled. Bunny was Kade's small dog who'd fallen head over heels for Iris. "I dunno. Sometimes I prefer dogs over people."

"Isn't that the truth," she agreed and then downed the rest of her drink. "I think you've convinced me. Are you sure you don't need me to stick around and help with cleanup?"

"I'm sure. Kennedy is going to come by later to help. Go. Love on the pup and put your feet up. Tomorrow we'll talk strategy to get more quality women signed up for our service." Most people tended to think it was harder to get men to join a dating service, but in my experience, it was always the women who were more reluctant. A lot of them had been burned in the past by men who expected them to manage all the emotional labor, household chores, and the majority of the child rearing, as well as finding a way to bring in a paycheck. Once the relationships ended, those women found themselves happier on their own.

And who could blame them? If they were already doing all the life work, why did they need another person to take care of all the time? It was my mission to set these women up with partners who would not only love them to pieces but also pull their weight when it came to dealing with everyday life.

"I think if we highlight the quality matches you've already made, it'll help," Iris said.

"Yeah, we need testimonials. Maybe a video, but we'll talk about that tomorrow. Go on and have a nice night." I eyed her empty glass. "Do you need me to call a car service?"

She shook her head. "Nah. I'm going to go take a walk down by the beach and then head home. Say hi to Jax for me when he gets here."

"Will do." I waved as she disappeared back into the restaurant and then turned my attention back to Brix. He was still talking to Tazia, and while she was smiling, it looked a bit forced. I had just taken my first step toward them when my dad appeared by her side. He placed his hand on her elbow and whispered something in Tazia's ear.

Tazia nodded once, said something to Brix, and then walked over to an empty table where she sat next to my father.

"It looks like my plan worked perfectly," Aunt Lucy said as she slid up next to me at the bar.

I grinned at my aunt. "When you're right you're right. Need a drink?"

"Do I ever. I'm getting parched talking to all these hot men. Where in the world did you find them?" She waved at a handful of seniors off in a corner. All three of them were dressed in suits, looking handsome, but one had chosen a burgundy, form-fitting suit with a white T-shirt underneath. The stylish man looked like an older version of Brendon Urie, and if I knew my aunt, he was the one she'd be picking for her first date.

"Trade secret," I said, handing her a dry martini, her usual drink of choice.

She giggled like a schoolgirl and took a sip. "I better get

back before they start fighting over me." With a wink, she hurried back over to her admirers.

I smiled to myself. There was nothing like the feeling when one of my mixers was a huge success. After checking to be sure Brix was mingling with a handful of successful women I'd invited to the mixer, I checked my phone for a text from Jax.

Nothing.

Sighing, I shoved the thing back in my pocket and was startled when I heard the loud pop of my favorite ghost appearing from thin air. My heart pounded against my ribcage as I jumped back and pressed a hand to my chest and glared. "Celia, dammit. Must you always do that? Wouldn't it be less conspicuous to walk in like a normal person?"

"I'm not normal. I wasn't even normal when I was alive," she said, waving a hand at herself. "Look at me. I'm a bobblehead with a body made for print modeling. I think I've worn just about every kind of underwear that has ever been made. Do you know what my favorites were?"

"None of them?" I asked, eyeing her suspiciously. "I think you told me once going commando was your preferred option."

Celia placed a hand on her chest and gave me heart eyes. "Oh. You listened to me. Now I'm all warm and fuzzy inside."

I rolled my eyes but grinned at her. If nothing else, Celia kept my days from being boring. "Did you find anything out at the field office?"

"No. Not one thing. I swear, it's like they're all robots. There wasn't even any chatter about the boss. It was as if she'd bugged the office or something and everyone was afraid to say anything. Do you have any idea how hard it was to stay incognito and not demand they tell me what the fuck was going on in that office?"

"Yes, I think I can imagine." Celia wasn't known for her patience. Persistence? Yes. She was worse than a dog with a bone when she wanted something, but to hang back and passively wait for information was likely torture for her.

"You're not going to make me go back there, are you?" she asked, her eyes pleading. "It's much more interesting hanging out at the construction site. Or even following Kennedy around. In both cases, I at least get a heavy dose of eye candy for my troubles."

I grimaced. "Kennedy is Ty's... person. Let's not refer to him as eye candy, okay?"

"You're no fun," the ghost complained.

"As far as keeping an eye on him, Skyler has that covered. And Jax has the construction site under control. Really, I need information from the field office. Surely you can start scanning documents to see what they're working on, right?"

"Ugh. I guess," she said, sounding more than a little put out.

"Thank you." I grinned at her, knowing that gratitude went a long way with Celia. "I appreciate it."

She immediately softened and gave me a playful eyeroll. "As long as you remember what a great employee I am, then you know I'll do whatever you need."

"You're the best," I said, appeasing her.

"You know it. Now, I'm going to mingle," she said. "See if I can find a hot guy to flirt with inside the restaurant."

"What about Danny?" I asked her. "How will he feel about you flirting with someone else?"

"Please." She blew out a short breath and laughed. "He spends all his evenings with drunk, horny women who love it when he flirts with them. What's good for the goose is good for the gander. Am I right?"

"Yep," I agreed. "Go have a good time. There's not much to

do here except wait for Brix to determine who he's most interested in anyway."

The ghost waggled her fingers and then disappeared into the building.

I spent the next few minutes making the rounds, checking to be sure Brix had met all the women I'd invited to the mixer. When I was satisfied, I checked on Aunt Lucy. She and the Brendon Urie look-alike had indeed made a connection and were on their way out for somewhere more private.

"Have fun," I told her. "Be safe. Say no to drinking and driving and yes to condoms."

She laughed and assured me that she'd only had half a drink and a pocketbook full of protection.

As they left together, I made my way back to the bar and asked for a cup of coffee. Just as the server handed me my cup, I spotted Tazia. She had an angry look on her face as she hastily walked away from my father. I glanced between them, noting that my dad looked frustrated but didn't make a move to follow her.

Shaking my head, I took a long sip of the coffee. Maybe it was time to accept the fact that Dad might just be a lost cause. Why would I want Tazia to keep putting up with his crap when I could find her someone who would appreciate everything she had to offer?

Tazia sidestepped a group of women and made a beeline for me.

"I'm sorry—" I started, but before I could get anything else out, she cut me off.

"I need to talk to you," she said, taking my elbow and leading me farther away from the crowd.

"If it's about my dad, then—"

"It's not." She shook her head. "Memphis is... Well, he has

some choices to make, but that's on him. Right now, I need to talk to you about Brix."

"Brix?" I glanced at my newest client and frowned. "What about him? It looked like you two were getting along before Dad started monopolizing your time."

"We were. He just..." She sighed. "Listen, remember when I told you there's someone in your life who isn't who they seem to be? I'm pretty sure Brix is that guy."

'What?" My eyes widened and then I eyed her with confusion. Every client we took on at my agency went through a thorough background check. I would not take the chance of setting someone up with anyone who might raise red flags. My top priority was to keep my clients safe. And Brix had passed with flying colors. Still, I trusted Tazia. If she had concerns, I wanted to hear them. "Why do you think that? What did he say to you?"

"It's not what he said." She glanced back at him before turning to me again. "It's that feeling I get. It was really strong. So strong that I—"

"Tazia?" my dad said, appearing behind her.

"Memphis, what—"

Without a word, Dad pulled her into his arms, dipped her backward, and kissed her with everything he had.

CHAPTER 20

I gaped at Dad and Tazia. There was no memory of my dad claiming anyone like that before, not even my own mother.

Tazia stiffened in his arms for a moment, and then all at once she just seemed to melt into him.

I blinked at them, practically frozen with shock.

"Memphis," Tazia said, pulling away from him slightly. "What's happening right now?"

He tightened his hold on her waist, pulled her in closer, and said, "I don't want this to end."

"The kiss?" she asked.

"No," he said. "This. What's happening between us. I don't want to lose you."

She placed her elegant hand over his heart and gave him a gentle smile. "I'm not sure we ever really started."

"That's not true and you know it. I've just been like I always am, pushing people away. I don't want to do that with you."

My heart swelled with pure joy as I watched my dad finally fight for someone he clearly wanted. Whatever she'd said to him before she'd come to talk to me, clearly it had lit a fire under his noncommittal ass. Good for her.

Tazia beamed at him. "Does this mean we're… dating?"

Dad nodded.

She raised her eyebrows in question. "Exclusively?"

There was no hesitation as he glanced at Brix and said, "Yes. Tell that guy you're taken."

She chuckled. "As long as you're aware that you are also off the market."

His lips twitched with amusement. "I've already disabled my online dating profile."

"Very classy, Dad," I said with a chuckle.

He gave me a pointed look. "I thought you'd be happy about this."

"I am. Very." I grinned at them. "Now go on. Take your date and go do something romantic."

"Wait," Tazia said, reaching out and placing a hand on my arm. "Just remember what I said about Brix."

"I will," I said, still confused about what it meant, but if she was adamant, I'd take her warning seriously.

With Tazia and my dad gone, I started making notes on which women seemed to be most compatible with Brix. Normally, I'd assess their auras, but since I'd been cursed a few weeks ago, that ability had vanished. Now I sometimes got that magical tingle at the base of my spine, but not always. Other times it was just a hunch.

I'd narrowed my picks down to three and was about to announce that the party was winding down when Kennedy appeared next to me. "Hey," I said, smiling at him. "You made it."

"I said I would." He glanced around. "What do you need me to do?"

"Could you start busing the tables? Just stack the glasses and plates for the caterers. They'll handle them from there."

"I'm on it." He gave me a small salute, grabbed a bussing bin from behind the bar, and got to work.

"Marion!" Celia gasped out as she floated right in front of me.

"Holy hell!" I jumped back, startled once again by the ghost.

"It's that jackass who spelled Kennedy." She pointed across the room.

I frowned at her before glancing around, trying to take everything in. "What do you mean? Is he here?"

"Yes!" She pointed toward Brix. "Right—oh shit!"

A tall, gangly, twenty-something man with a scar on his right cheek brushed past Brix, slightly nudging his shoulder.

"Did you see that?" Celia asked before she zoomed across the patio. "You little bastard. What did you put in Brix's drink?"

Brix glanced down at his drink and frowned.

"It was a pill." Celia circled Vince, moving so fast she was starting to resemble the Tasmanian Devil.

I ran over to Brix's side, grabbed the cup and sniffed the contents, surprised to find there was no hint of alcohol. "Diet Coke?" I asked him.

He nodded. "I switched an hour ago."

Nodding, I continued to inspect the cup, trying to determine whether Celia had just saved the day or if she was off her rocker.

Brix took the cup back and dropped a white pill into it. The contents immediately turned green and started to ooze.

"What the ever-loving hell?" I exclaimed. There was no doubt about it. Vince had tried to poison Brix by spiking his cup.

Vince took off toward the beach, but one of the women got in the way, and he ran into her, knocking them both down. He scrambled to his feet, only to come face to face with Brix.

Brix struck, landing a closed-fist blow to the man's face. Vince spun and came up fighting with a silver dagger in his hand.

I let out a gasp and reached for my bag, my fingers itching to be wrapped around my own dagger. When I opened my bag, the blue light from the weapon lit the night, and as soon as I wrapped my fingers around the handle, magic tingled up my arm.

"Marion!" Kennedy cried and came to stand right next to me. "What are you doing?"

"I'm making sure nothing happens to Brix, that's what," I said, springing into action. I wasn't sure what made me do it. I wasn't exactly the type to run into danger. But the magic coursing through me had taken on a life of its own, and no one was going to hurt one of my guests. "Drop it. Now!" I called, pointing my dagger at Vince.

Vince glanced at me once and then dismissed me with a roll of his eyes.

"Marion," Brix said under his breath. "I've got this handled."

"It sure doesn't look like it."

Vince lunged at me, but before I could engage, Brix kicked out, hitting his arm right in the elbow. Vince let out a cry of pain but didn't drop his weapon. Instead, he jumped toward me, only to be headed off by Kennedy, who rammed into him with his shoulder, sending the slender man backward into a table.

Wood splintered as the women cried out and scattered. Vince had barely hit the ground before he was back on his feet, already coming for Kennedy. "You were the biggest disappointment. I offered you a life of independence and more money than your sorry ass has ever seen, and what did you do? You got caught and almost got us both dragged off to jail. You're lucky I didn't hunt you down and gut you after that just for being an inconvenience."

"You offered me a place to stay and a job as a laborer in a landscaping business. Nowhere in our agreement was an expectation to steal from the people of Premonition Pointe," Kennedy countered.

"*Pfft.* What the hell did you think you were going to get paid the big money for? Pulling weeds? Come on, man. You can't be that stupid."

I placed my hand on Kennedy's arm. "Don't engage with him."

Kennedy glanced at my dagger. "I could say the same to you."

Brix grabbed Vince's wrist and twisted, but Vince must have been trained in hand-to-hand combat, because he quickly and efficiently elbowed Brix in the gut with his other arm and then yanked himself free with enough momentum that he barreled into Kennedy, sending them both to the ground. Before Kennedy could get his bearings, Vince already had his arm around Kennedy and his dagger pressed against the exposed part of his neck.

Kennedy's eyes were wide with fear as he froze.

"Let Kennedy go," I said calmly.

Vince just laughed. "Hell no. This asshole is my ticket out of here."

Brix glanced between me and Kennedy before taking a step toward Vince and his hostage.

"One more step, old man, and I'll slice his neck open," Vince threatened. In fact, he was pressing the knife so hard against Kennedy's skin that he'd already started to bleed.

"Get back," I ordered Brix. "Do what he says."

Brix held both hands up in surrender.

I could see by the look in Vince's eyes that he was considering going after Brix right then and there, intending to finish the job he'd started. But Kennedy struck out at him, smashing Vince's knee with his foot.

"Fuck!" Vince called out and then punched Kennedy in the kidney. "Do that again, and the next time it will be my knife."

Sirens sounded off in the distance, causing Vince to tighten his grip on Kennedy. "You're my ticket out of here, jackass. Now move!"

"No!" I cried as panic finally started to take over. "Let Kennedy go. Take me," I offered stupidly.

Celia jumped in front of me. "You're not taking her, you dirtbag. You're not taking Kennedy either." She lunged for him, but her ethereal body just dissipated into tiny particles when she reached for him.

Vince visibly shivered but then brushed it off and pushed Kennedy forward. "Move your feet, or I'll make sure you can never move them again. Got it?"

Kennedy muttered something about me staying safe and then did as Vince told him and let the other man frog-march him off the patio and into the dark night.

As soon as they disappeared onto the beach, Brix and I both sprang into action. I took off after them with my glowing dagger and enough rage to fuel an entire power plant. That little criminal had just abducted Kennedy. No way in hell was I just going to leave that to the authorities. I was determined to bring Kennedy home if it was the last thing I did.

"Marion, go back to the party," Brix ordered. "You have no idea what you're dealing with."

"And you do?" I countered as I narrowed my eyes, scrutinizing him. "What would a real estate investor know about tracking criminals?"

He grumbled something unintelligible and took off down the beach.

I paused, closed my eyes, and listened. The magical tingle in my lower back had spread. The magic was pulsing through my body, urging me to run. To fight. To stop at nothing until I had Kennedy back home safe where he should be.

But when I tried to move my feet, I found I was stuck in the sand, unable to do anything. It was as if I were cemented into the sand, and I wasn't going anywhere. I let out a cry of pure frustration as hot angry tears rolled down my cheeks.

"Marion? You called?" Celia asked.

My eyes sprung open, and if it had been possible, I'd have hugged the hell out of the ghost. "You need to find help. Someone from the restaurant. My feet are buried and I need help getting out of here."

Celia looked more than a little skeptical as she glanced around at the deserted beach. "I can't leave you out here alone," she said, shaking her head. "What if that asshole Vince comes back?"

"Then it will give me a chance to slice his balls off," I said, swiping my still glowing blade in the air. I paused and really stared at the dagger. The blue magic intensified until it was a deep sapphire hue and the magic took on a life of its own.

"Okay. I'll be right back. Don't get eaten or kidnapped while I go find help," Celia said, sounding worried. It was rare for the ghost to show her fears. That's how I knew I was in a world of hurt.

Celia disappeared once more, leaving me alone in the darkness. I stared at my gleaming dagger until my limbs were vibrating as if the magic was willing me to do something. Anything.

"Fine!" I cried out in desperation and then used the dagger to form a circle around my feet. Magic crackled from the edge of the blade and into the groove of the circle I'd made.

"Marion?" a feminine voice called from the night shadows. "Are you all right?"

I glanced in the direction of the voice and squinted, but I couldn't make out more than the form of the woman coming toward me. I clutched my dagger harder, knowing if the shit hit the fan it was the only thing that might save me.

"I'm armed!" I called out. "Don't come any closer."

"I know," the woman said, not making any effort to stop. "I can tell you're scared. Just breathe. Like meditation to calm down. I have information you want."

She did?

I tried to shift my feet, but my boots wouldn't budge. Despite the magical ring I was locked in, I felt a sense of power that was still heavily radiating from the dagger.

The woman stopped right in front of me, her face suddenly visible in the sliver of moonlight and the ambient light from my dagger. She looked so familiar, but I couldn't quite place her. Her long silver-gray hair fell down her back in waves, and her eyes were accented by crow's feet and full of wisdom.

"Angela Anderson," the woman said, holding her hand out to me.

I quickly took it with my free hand and squeezed as my brain made the connection. Angela was Hope's mother, and she could read minds.

"I have important information for you," she said.

"About Kennedy?" I asked, giving up on my boots. It was clear the only way I was walking away from this was to ditch them. Grimacing at the idea of leaving my leather boots behind in the sand, I unzipped them and pulled my feet out of the magical circle. I loved those boots. But I loved my freedom more.

"It's about Jax's construction site," she said simply.

I jerked my head up, staring at her. "What about it?" My heart started racing again, and anxiety kicked in. But I didn't have time for any of that. Kennedy had just been abducted, and Angela was standing in front of me, determined to tell me what she'd heard. Sleep would be impossible until Kennedy was safe, so I might as well go hunt him down myself. There was no time to wait.

"I know who bombed it," Angela said.

"Who?" I gave her my full and undivided attention.

She jerked her head toward the beach. "That guy's name is Vince, right?"

I nodded, swallowing to try to dislodge the boulder clogging my throat.

"It was him. He did it at the direction of his boss."

"Who's his boss?" I asked.

"Someone named Agent Erikson."

I let out a loud gasp. "Agent Erikson from the Magical Task Force?"

"Yes. That's the one," Angela said. "I tried to get you more details, but the restaurant is busier than I thought it was going to be, and the noise drowned out a lot of his thoughts."

"That's... more than enough. Thank you, Angela." I ran from the beach back up to the street to find my car and pressed the phone to my ear, trying to call Jax. He needed to know immediately that the people who were investigating his case were in on a cover-up. What else were they doing? Dread coiled in my belly when Jax didn't answer. I left a quick message and then dialed again just in case he hadn't heard the first one.

When he didn't answer, I started calling coven members.

Busy signal.

"Dammit, Iris. Where are you?" I asked and then hung up. It was the same with the other coven members. Again. A coil of dread took up residence in my gut. How was it possible this was happening again? Only this time, I didn't even have Hollister by my side.

Fuck.

CHAPTER 21

*B*arefoot and chilled to the bone from the wind coming off the ocean, I jumped into my SUV, grateful that I'd kept the key in my pocket. I'd left the mixer with only my phone, the dagger, and the key to my vehicle. It was enough. I'd get my bag later.

With shaking hands, I pulled the SUV out of the parking lot, determined to find the members of the coven before I did anything else. Without knowing where Vince had taken Kennedy, we needed to do a finding spell as soon as possible. I pressed on the gas and headed for Gigi's house since it was the closest.

But before I could make the turn onto her street, a black SUV cut me off, forcing me to slam on the breaks before I crashed right into the other vehicle. My dagger flared to life, bathing my car in its blue light. I grabbed it, welcoming the magic that surged into me. Determined not to be a sitting duck, I jumped out of my SUV, wielding my dagger and more than ready to use it if anyone came for me.

"I warned you to stay out of this," said a voice from the darkness.

"Stay out of what exactly?" I all but snarled, hating that I couldn't see my adversary. "All I was doing was hosting a mixer when that piece of shit criminal came and tried to kill my client."

"Don't play dumb, Marion. You sent that ghost to spy on the Magical Task Force. Did you think we didn't know?"

My heart thundered against my ribcage. *Shit.* I wasn't going to be able to bluff my way out of this one. "I can't control what Celia does."

"She's your employee."

I didn't bother to deny it. There was no point in arguing. "What do you want from me?"

"Get in the SUV," he ordered. "I'm taking you to see the boss."

"Hell no. You've lost your fucking mind if you think I'm going anywhere with you."

A bolt of magic crackled through the night and on instinct, I raised the dagger, shielding my heart. The magic hit the dagger's blade, sending me stumbling backward into the side of my SUV from the force of it. My arm vibrated and the handle of the dagger heated up to an almost unbearable degree, but I held on for dear life, certain that if I moved even a fraction his magic would kill me.

"Drop it!" he ordered, stepping closer. My attacker wore a hoodie that shielded his face, ripped jeans, and work boots. The kind that one would find on a construction site.

"Who are you?" I demanded.

"The person who's going to end you." He increased the intensity of the magic. I held the dagger with two hands, trying to keep it in place, but I was losing steam. My muscles were weakening and if something didn't change quickly, I was going to lose this battle sooner rather than later.

Kennedy's image popped into my mind, and suddenly a fierce determination overtook me. I pushed the dagger away from my chest and pointed it in my assailant's direction, imagining the magic bouncing back toward him. To my surprise, the magic did just that as my entire body vibrated with the effort.

"Fuck!" he cried and threw himself headfirst into the bushes to his left.

There was no hesitation as I jumped back into my SUV and slammed it into reverse. The tires squealed as I quickly backed up and spun the wheel, intending to hightail it out of there as fast as I could.

Boom!

My car rocked, bouncing me so that my head hit the roof and then settled with the car listing to the right. "Oh, crap." The hair rose on the back of my neck, and I just knew the mysterious guy was going to be standing right outside.

My door jerked open and a hand reached in, grabbing my arm.

I jabbed my dagger blindly at my attacker, only to have another hand wrap around my wrist, stopping me.

"Marion. Stop!" A familiar voice ordered. "It's me, Brix."

"Let go!" I struggled to free myself, still gripping my dagger for dear life.

He released me and stepped back, holding his hands up. "I'm here to help you."

"By blowing out my tires? What the hell kind of help is that?" I scoffed.

"That wasn't me." He waved at the black SUV still parked in front of me. "It was him."

I squinted and finally spotted the outline of a man laid out flat on the pavement. "Did you do that?" I asked Brix.

"Yes. He was trying to blow up your car." He held his hand out to me. "Come on. You need to get out of here before he comes to."

I glanced between the two men, not at all sure what I should do. On the one hand, the unconscious man had just attacked me and my SUV. On the other, Tazia had been right about Brix. He'd clearly lied about who he was, and I just didn't trust him.

The man on the pavement moaned and started to stir.

"Marion, come on." Brix reached for me, but I brushed his hand away.

"I can get out under my own steam, thank you very much." I stumbled out of the vehicle only to be grabbed around the waist and pulled out of the way before another lightning bolt of magic blasted right into me.

Brix quickly put me down and stood in front of me, shielding me with his body.

"You piece of shit," the man near the black SUV snarled at him. "The only reason you're alive right now is because the boss ordered it. But that doesn't mean I can't make you suffer before I hog tie you and haul you back to the compound."

"You could try." There was ice in Brix's voice as he stalked toward the man.

Another bolt of magic lit up the night, and I widened my eyes in surprise as Brix just held up his hand and seemed to collect the magic in his palm before sending it back at the man. It hit him squarely in the chest, causing the man to instantly go limp.

"Holy hell," I breathed. "Is he dead?"

Brix walked over to him, pressed two fingers to his pulse point on his neck, and then shook his head as he pulled zip ties out of his back pocket. "Unfortunately, no." Brix quickly secured the man's wrists together and then moved on to his ankles. "Marion, check his SUV for a phone or anything suspicious."

I hesitated for just a moment, not at all sure I wanted to look in the other vehicle. What if there was another person lying in wait?

"Marion! The more time we waste, the harder it will be to find Kennedy."

That got me moving. If Brix was going to help me find Kennedy, I'd have to trust him now and ask questions later.

He bent over the unconscious man and started searching his pockets. I gathered my courage and peeked inside the black SUV. Thankfully, it was empty except for a small silver case that had an amulet, a ceremonial knife, and a variety of herbs. None of which I dared touch with my bare hands. Instead, I closed the case, grabbed a phone that was sitting on the console, and retreated to the black Jeep that was parked diagonally in the street.

Brix jumped into the driver's side, and within seconds we were peeling away from the scene of the crime. He glanced over at me. "You okay?"

I narrowed my eyes at him. "Who are you?"

He nodded once. "Definitely okay if you're asking that question."

"I'm fine. Answer the question." I turned to face him, watching his profile as he sped down the streets of Premonition Pointe.

"I'm Brixton Belford. But you can call me Brix." He gave me an easy smile that made me want to deck him.

"Stop the fucking car," I demanded.

"No can do. We're tracking Vince." He pointed to his phone mounted on the dash.

At first glance, I'd thought it was just mapping software. But as I looked closer, I spotted a flashing dot that was moving north up the coastline. We were a good twenty miles behind. My heart got caught in my throat. If he was tracking Vince, that meant we were tracking Kennedy, too. "How are you tracking him? And why?"

Brix ran a hand over his jaw, and suddenly the man looked exhausted. He glanced at me. "The tracking device is a trick of the trade. As for why I'm tracking him, I'd think that was obvious. The guy works for the biggest crime boss in the area. I've been working for months to get evidence to bring his boss down. The only way to get to the ringleader is through his grunt workers."

My eyes widened, and although I was still in flight mode, I took a couple of deep breaths, trying to calm myself. Brix's background check had been wholly unremarkable. But if he had magic and was able to track criminals, then the information I'd dug up on him had been a complete lie. Trusting him would be insanity. At the same time, if he really was tracking Vince and Kennedy, he was my best hope of saving the young man I'd come to care about so much in such a short time.

"I'm going to need more than that," I said, positioning my dagger on my lap so that it was more accessible should I need to use it on the man. "Are you a vigilante? Working for law enforcement? A jilted lover?"

He smirked. "Definitely not a jilted lover. Though I like the thoroughness of your line of questioning."

"Stop fucking with me," I said with a sigh. "I need to know right now if you're a good guy or a bad guy."

"What do you think?" he asked, raising one eyebrow.

The tingle started at the base of my spine again, though I wasn't sure what that meant. That happened when I was around Hollister, too. I trusted Hollister. Did that mean I should trust this guy?

Hell no.

He'd have to earn my trust. "I think two things. One, that you saved my ass from whoever the hell that was back there. And two, you claim to be tracking Vince. That's plausible since the man tried to poison you. And Kennedy is likely with him. That leaves me no choice but to go along with you so that I can bring him home. Otherwise, I'd be fighting a lot harder to get out of this vehicle."

He nodded. "Good."

"Good? What the hell does that mean? *Good.* Nothing is going to be good until you level with me."

His lips twitched as if he were holding back a smile. "Tell me this, Marion Matched. If I told you I was a former agent for the Magical Task Force and that I'd gone rogue to bring down a bad actor, what would you say?"

An eerie shiver ran down my spine. "Is that true?"

He slowed to make a turn onto a dark highway and shrugged one shoulder. "I'm not saying it is and I'm not saying it isn't. However, you're smack in the middle of a shit storm and you're going to have to trust someone. Who's it going to be? Me or the man who tried to obliterate you back there on the streets of Premonition Pointe?"

"Those choices suck," I muttered.

"I'm sure they do. Mine haven't been rock solid choices either. But here we are. Do you want to find Kennedy or not?"

"Yes," I said without hesitation.

"Great. Keep that dagger out." He pressed his foot on the gas and sped up as he rounded a corner. "You're going to need it."

CHAPTER 22

"This is where we're stopping?" I asked Brix as I stood at the edge of a bluff, looking over an abandoned ghost town. There were three buildings, one that had been a gas station at one point, a dilapidated inn, and a boarded-up shack that still had a large sign that was barely visible in the moonlight. The white letters read *Rosie's*.

"Vince is here." He glanced down at his phone. "In Rosie's."

"How do you know that?" I asked. "I don't see his car. He could be anywhere."

"He's in Rosie's," Brix said again and showed me the flashing light on his device. If his tracker was accurate, the little criminal was indeed inside that building.

"Okay. If you say so." I bit down on my lower lip. "I don't like this. It's too... quiet. Too remote. It feels like a trap."

"What does your magic say?" he asked as he walked to his vehicle and pulled out the amulet and small ceremonial knife from the case we'd taken from my attacker.

I glanced down at my dagger. It was as ordinary as could be. No blue light in sight. "Nothing, I guess."

"Exactly. You have a gift, Marion. If there was magic nearby, you'd know it."

Was that true? Was that why my dagger glowed blue so often? Premonition Pointe was full of magic. We had our own coven for the goddess's sake. But out here? It was just me and Brix... and maybe Vince and Kennedy if we were lucky. "I don't know what you're talking about."

"Yes you do." He rummaged around in his Jeep while I took my phone out and checked for a signal.

Nothing. I'd tried numerous times to call Jax and members of the coven while we'd been on the road, but I'd either been left with no service or I'd gotten that dreaded busy signal again. It didn't escape me that I was out in the woods with a man I knew nothing about, tracking a criminal who'd abducted Kennedy and had attempted to murder Brix less than a couple hours ago.

I was a matchmaker, not a super hero. How the hell was I always getting into these messes?

Shaking my head, I focused on what I had to do in order to bring Kennedy home.

"You ready?" Brix asked me.

I nodded and followed the man down a trail that led into town.

Brix used the flashlight from his phone to illuminate the trail, and I quickly did the same, being careful not to trip over exposed roots. The last thing we needed was for one of us to sprain an ankle before we ever even confronted Vince.

Once we were on flat land, we both turned off our lights and pocketed our phones. I'd taken pains to silence mine even though it still wasn't showing any service. It would be just my luck that a text would come through and expose our position as we were sneaking up on him.

"Do you feel it?" Brix asked in a low voice.

"Feel what?" I asked.

"The magic. It's here in the air."

Now that I was focusing, I nodded. "Yes. My lower back is tingling. That's where I feel it first." I tapped the handle of my dagger and each time I touched it, the blade lit with blue light.

Brix's gaze dropped to the dagger and then narrowed. When he looked up again, he stared into my eyes, seemingly searching for something.

"What?"

"Just thinking. Don't worry about it. I'm going to go around the back. You stay at the front door. If Vince tries to escape, don't hesitate to take him down."

I blinked at Brix. "Take him down? Do you have me confused with someone else? I've taken a self-defense class a time or two, but I'm hardly trained in magical combat."

"You certainly were holding your own earlier with that dagger of yours," he said.

I wrapped my hand around the hilt, recalling how I'd deflected my attacker's magic. "I was a badass, wasn't I?"

He chuckled softly. "That you were. Just be on guard. If he runs, don't hesitate to stop him."

"But—" Before I could get the rest of the sentence out, Brix had already taken off across the deserted road and was headed toward the back of the building. I suddenly felt very alone. If something happened to Brix or we got separated, I was completely on my own. No car. No phone service. No idea how to get back to town.

Panic started to coil in my belly and my vision blurred. But I tightened my grip on the dagger, and the world came back into focus. Determination pushed the panic down. There was no way I was going to play the role of a damsel in distress. Not now. Not ever.

Silently, I made my way across to the rundown building. Once I was pressed up against the wall next to the front door, I could just make out the sound of soft music from inside. It was what one might expect when they were waiting on hold to get through to someone on the phone. Why was Vince listening to elevator music? A shiver ran down my spine, and suddenly I had an overwhelming sense of wrongness. I automatically gripped the hilt of my dagger, and the blade lit with blue light.

I had to find Brix. It was unsafe. We were in—

Boom!

I dove to the dirt, curling in on myself as I covered my head with my arms. Wood and glass rained down on me, and I let out a loud grunt as pain seared into my shoulder and down my back.

Dust filled the air, and I squinted, trying to see through the destruction. The sound of boots crunching on debris had me trying to scramble up into a sitting position, but when I moved, my shoulder seized as the unbearable pain rendered me motionless.

"Marion?" Brix asked. "Are you all right?"

The fear that had taken up residence in my chest eased at the sound of his voice. "You're alive." It was a statement, not a question.

"So are you. Can you move?" He was covered in soot and had a wound on his head, but he didn't appear to be injured otherwise.

I shook my head. "Not easily. What exactly is impaled in my shoulder?"

"A piece of glass."

"Fuck. We can't just yank that out. I'll need a healer," I said, wondering how the hell I was going to keep looking for Kennedy if I couldn't even move until I found someone to stitch me up.

"Good thing we have one, then," he said and kneeled down beside me.

"What? Where?"

He gave me a whisper of a smile. "You're looking at him. Give me just a second, and I'll fix you right up."

"You're a healer?" I asked in disbelief.

"That's what the sign on the door says." He reached into the inside of his jacket and pulled out the small ceremonial knife we'd taken from my attacker.

"What are you going to do with that?"

"You'll see." He stood, held the knife out in front of him with two hands, closed his eyes, and muttered a few words I couldn't make out. The knife flashed red and then pure white. His eyes popped open and he nodded. Then, without any warning, he yanked the piece of glass out of my shoulder.

I let out a cry and nearly threw up from the intensity of the pain. But when he pressed the knife to the wound, the nausea vanished and all I felt was the heat from the knife where it rested against my skin.

"This might hurt a little," he said.

"What are you—ouch! Son of a mother-effing ballsack!" The heat of the knife turned to pure fire, making my flesh burn and my muscles tremble from the intrusion. "What the fuck are you doing to me?"

"It's a crude method, but by the time I'm done, there will be no chance of infection and your flesh will have already started mending," he said in a matter-of-fact tone.

"Son of a bitch." I bit down on the sleeve of my jacket and tried not to scream through the agony.

Finally, the searing pain faded and the area started to itch like mad.

"Brix?" I said through clenched teeth. "How long is this itching going to last?"

"It could be five minutes or a day or two. It all depends on how fast you heal. Come on. We need to go."

I pushed myself to my feet and stood in front of him. "Where are we headed?"

He reached into his pocket and pulled out a piece of fabric. On closer inspection, I realized it was a blood-stained rag. "Place the tip of your dagger on this."

"Why?" I asked, staring at the offending piece of fabric.

"Because, Marion, Vince dislodged the tracker that was in his arm and left this as a gift. When I picked it up, it set off the bombs that decimated this place. If it hadn't been for my magic, I'd have lost my hand at the very least, maybe even a couple of limbs."

"You... your magic saved you?" I asked, dumbfounded.

"It's called a magic shield. One day when this is over, I'll teach it to you. But for now, I need you to touch that dagger to this rag."

"Again, why?" I asked.

"Because as soon as you do, your dagger will tell us where we need to go."

CHAPTER 23

*B*rix wasn't entirely correct when he'd said my dagger would tell us where to find Vince. While the dagger ignited a magical connection, it wasn't the weapon itself that was signaling where we had to go.

It was me.

The moment the tip of the dagger hit the blood, I felt a tug in my gut. And the tug was telling me I needed to go east.

"That way." I started walking down the middle of the street, marveling at my new power.

"Marion, we need to get the Jeep," Brix said.

I glanced up the side of the hill and grimaced. "You think it's that far?"

"You really think it isn't? There's nothing else around here except these three buildings." He didn't wait for me. He just took off up the path, and I had no choice but to follow him even though every molecule in my body wanted to head east down that dark road.

By the time we made it to the top of the hill, I was almost

doubled over in physical pain due to moving in the opposite direction of Vince.

Brix yanked the passenger side door open and lifted me in.

"Thanks," I grunted.

He didn't say anything as he ran back to his side, jumped in, and sped down the hill. As soon as we were headed in the correct direction, the pain eased and I started to breathe easier.

"This spell you put on me is a bitch," I said.

He glanced over. "What spell?"

"The one that is pointing us in the direction of Vince."

"I didn't spell you. I thought you understood that it's the magic in your dagger that gave you that ability."

"That's not possible," I said automatically.

"Why not?"

"I…" Why couldn't it be possible? Did I really have any idea what the dagger could do other than be a defense against a magical attack? Did that mean the dagger that had claimed me gave me access to all kinds of magic?

"I didn't know I could render Marion Matched speechless," he said with a small chuckle.

"I'm not speechless. Just thinking." I held the dagger up, inspecting it. "A friend told me this dagger claimed me. I haven't had it very long, and since it didn't come with an instruction manual, I think it's safe to say I have no idea what all it can do. But I think you might be able to shed some light on that."

"I might." He slowed at a fork in the road. "Which way?"

"Right," I said.

He eased onto the deserted road. "The dagger by itself isn't all that special. It's useful for spells and rituals as well as helping the owner be a little quicker on their feet in any sort of battle. But when it chooses someone, when it melds with a

HONOR-BOUND WITCH

witch's power source, it can do all kinds of things that effectively make its owner an extremely powerful witch."

I gaped at him. "I'm not powerful. Up until a few weeks ago, all I could really do was read auras. Now…" I shrugged. "It seems I can do a few things, but only if I'm holding this."

"A few things?" He chuckled. "Because of you and that dagger, we're about to break the case of the decade and maybe save a few lives in the process. Classifying its power as being able to do 'a few things' is understating the power just a tad, don't you think?"

"The case of the decade?" I asked. What the hell had Kennedy walked into? "Brix, you have some serious explaining to do."

"I'll explain everything after."

"After what?"

He pointed just ahead of us to where the road dead-ended. There was a gated property with a large *No Trespassing* sign on it, and he parked the Jeep right in front of it.

"Uh, Brix, don't you think we should turn around and park this thing somewhere a little less conspicuous?"

"It's too late," he said. "There are cameras all over this section. They already know we're here."

I quickly glanced around, looking for… Well, I wasn't sure what I was looking for. An ambush maybe? My body was on full alert as I climbed out of the Jeep and followed Brix over the gate.

"No matter what happens, do not drop or give up that dagger. It will likely save your life. Got it?"

I gripped the dagger and had the fleeting thought that I should run in the other direction. What was I doing, just walking on to private property that was by all account inhabited by criminals?

Kennedy.

His shy smile flashed in my mind along with his curious eyes, and that was all I needed to keep putting one foot in front of the other. I refused to give up the search until I found him.

This would not be like Kiera. My heart squeezed painfully, and I had to push aside my guilt about giving up on looking for her. I'd had my reasons. It had been an impossible choice, one that would always make me uncomfortable.

"This way," Brix said, pulling me behind a row of sequoia trees.

"He's that way," I said, pointing in the opposite direction.

"I know. That's why we're going the other direction. We need to find a place where we can get the lay of the land."

"That won't be necessary," a deep voice said from behind us.

We both spun and then froze when we spotted the gun aimed right at us.

"It's Brix now, right?" the man said.

"Obviously you already know the answer to that, Derek," Brix said.

"Just wanted to make sure. It's not every day a man runs into his brother who disappeared seven years ago and changed his identity."

Brother? What the hell?

"It's not every day that a man finds out his brother is the most corrupt motherfucker in the Magical Task Force agency either. I guess we all have to learn to live with disappointment."

"Magical Task Force?" I whispered.

"Marion, meet my brother, Agent Derek Erikson of the Magical Task Force. He oversees all the highest profile cases. Which is a convenient way to cover up his multitude of crimes."

Agent Erikson? The same Erikson who was overseeing the bombing of Jax's construction site?

"Why are we airing all our dirty laundry in front of your friend?" Erikson asked in a sickly-sweet tone.

"You started it," Brix said.

Erikson laughed. "It's just like when we were boys. Are you going to tattle to Mom now?"

"Don't you dare talk about my mother," Brix growled. And then despite the gun, he launched himself at Erikson. The two men went down in a heap of arms and legs as they wrestled, each doing his best to strangle the other one.

I took a step back, watching warily and praying that Brix came out the victor of their scuffle. But I wasn't going to stand around and wait to see the result. There was a solid chance that Kennedy was here at this house, and the sooner I found him the better. I spun on my heel, only turning back once to find Brix straddling his brother, both hands wrapped around his neck as he ordered him to never speak of their mother again.

A chill ran down my spine. The hatred between the two brothers was palpable. Whatever had happened, the intensely negative feelings between them were mutual.

Brix's head snapped up and his eyes caught mine. He only said one word. "Go!"

This time, I didn't look back.

CHAPTER 24

*With my dagger clasped in my hand, I ran for all I was worth toward the large farmhouse. Lights lit a pathway to the front door, and there was a large *Welcome* sign on the porch. To anyone who stumbled onto the place, it would look warm and welcoming, which was odd considering the giant *No Trespassing* sign on the gates out front.

But I didn't head to the front door. Instead, I skirted around the detached garage and made my way around the back. That pull toward the house was stronger than it had ever been, indicating that Vince was inside. I held onto hope that it meant I'd find Kennedy in there, too.

There was movement near the backdoor, causing me to duck behind a large box van parked behind the garage and catch my breath. I crept along the side, my heart racing, but then I stopped in my tracks when I noticed a familiar logo on the van.

No. Not a van. A food truck.

It was hard to make out in the darkness, but there it was. That stylized J that Tandy had asked her assistant to track down. I pressed my hand to my throat as I tried to put the pieces together. Why would this food truck be in the yard of Agent Erikson's house?

The light around my dagger brightened, and the tingle that had been buzzing at my spine intensified. The magic swirling inside me made it difficult to stand still. I had to move, do something, anything to find Kennedy. But just as soon as I'd made up my mind to storm the house, I spotted a blue Honda Accord parked right next to the food truck.

Kiera?

I was certain Hollister had told me that was the type of car she drove. I hurried over to it, noting the thin layer of dust that covered it. It hadn't been moved in days. After glancing around, I opened the passenger side door and peered inside. The overhead light lit the car, illuminating a gently used vehicle with a white fast food paper bag with a J on the side crumpled on the floorboard. That was more than enough to confirm it had to be Kiera's car.

Tears stung my eyes unexpectantly, but I blinked them back. This was no time to cry. Not when I was this close to finding my friend. All that stuff about her being wanted for manslaughter meant nothing to me. Not after I'd just learned one of the big dogs of the agency was one of the worst criminal offenders out there. How could I trust anything anyone from the MTF said?

My fingers itched to call Jax. To warn him. But still, there was no phone service. No wonder Erikson had chosen this location for his lair. Remote and inaccessible was exactly what he needed when he was keeping people against their will.

I grabbed the photo of Garrison, stuffed it in my pocket, and then darted toward the house.

"Hello, Marion," a familiar female voice said.

I jerked to a stop. "Kiera?"

"I knew you'd find me somehow," she said, sounding sad and dejected.

I scanned the back porch, searching frantically for her. Finally my gaze landed on a chair sitting in the shadows next to the back door. "Have you been here the entire time you've been missing?"

"Ever since my ex's goons abducted me," she said.

I wanted to run to her. To wrap my arms around her and tell her it was going to be okay now. That whatever had happened, if there were still charges, we'd find a way to get them dropped. That she'd be going back to Garrison and that all of this would be over.

But something held me back. I didn't know what it was. It was just a feeling that I needed to keep my distance.

Run! A voice sounded in my head.

"Kiera?" I asked, taking a step backward.

"I'm right here, Marion. You just need to come untie me."

Lies! The voice in my head cried. *That's not me. Do not listen to her!*

Kiera? I replied in my head. *Is that you?*

Yes. I'm upstairs in the far right window. Look up when you get a chance.

"Kiera," I said to the person on the porch. "Why wait around? You come to me and we'll get out of here right now."

"I can't. I'm tied to this chair," the woman on the porch said. "I need you to rescue me."

"Rescue you?" I parroted, but only because they were words I was certain Kiera would never use. She wasn't a girl who ever waited around for someone to rescue her. She'd take the bull by the horns and do it herself.

"Please, Marion." The voice sounded so broken and pathetic

I almost caved. But then I glanced up and spotted Kiera. She was standing in the window, staring down at me with a determined expression.

It was an expression I'd seen countless times.

Tell him Derek's hurt, Kiera said through our connection.

It probably wasn't a total lie. When I'd left Brix and Derek, they'd been trying to kill each other. *I can't*, I replied. *If I send him to Erikson, there's a good chance it'll end up two on one. I can't do that to Brix.*

You have to, Marion. You have to clear the way so you can get Kennedy out of here.

Kennedy?

He's here and if you don't get him now, they'll kill him.

That was it. I didn't hesitate. "Derek's hurt," I blurted to the fake Kiera. "Back there toward the trees. If someone doesn't get to him soon, he's going to bleed out."

There was an abrupt movement on the porch, and suddenly Vince was bathed in light as he stormed back into the house.

I ran around to a side door that I was certain must lead to the kitchen. When I heard the front door slam and heavy boots on the porch, I carefully opened the door and slipped into the house. That urge to follow Vince was still strong, but my desire to find Kennedy and Kiera was stronger.

After checking to be sure there weren't any bodyguards nearby, I dashed through the kitchen and up the stairs, making a beeline for Kiera's room. Just before I reached her door, the one next to it flew open, and I rammed into it head first.

"Fuck!" I cried.

"Did you really think I'd fall for your bullshit?" Vince said, towering over me.

I stared up at him and into his soulless dark eyes that were lit with rage. "Did you really think you'd get away with killing Brix and abducting Kennedy?"

"You two troublemakers are done, do you hear me? Done. I may not have succeeded in ending that traitor's life, but Derek will get it done. Mark my words. There will be one less Erikson brother in the world tonight."

My skin crawled, and I had an undeniable urge to spit in this guy's face. He wasn't the kind of person who engaged in criminal behavior because he needed the money or out of some misguided attempt at loyalty. No, Vince did it because he liked it. Craved it, probably.

"What? Does that make you queasy, princess?" he said with a sardonic laugh.

"No, but you do," I said as I grabbed him and jabbed my knee into his groin, putting as much force behind the attack as I could muster. As soon as he grunted and curled forward, I slammed my elbow down on his shoulder and grinned when I heard the sickening pop of his shoulder being dislocated. "Try to attack me with one arm, asshole," I hissed and then threw him against the wall. "That was payback for making me slam my head into the door."

"I did you a favor, now you can get a nose job on your insurance's dime," he said as if he hadn't felt a thing.

Hell, maybe he hadn't. There were spells out there that made a person immune to pain for a short time. If he had activated something to block his pain receptors, he was going to be in a world of hurt when the spell wore off.

"You'll never free her from here, you know," he went on, grinning at me with a maniacal expression. "She's bound to Derek." He shot a look of disgust at the last room. "The bitch doesn't deserve him."

"Oh, that's how it is then? You jealous she has ties to the man you want?" I taunted.

"Fuck you. I'm not into dick." He curled up against the wall and closed his eyes. The pain was finally starting to settle in.

As fun as it was to antagonize the man and beat the shit out of him for what he'd done, my bigger priorities were Kennedy and Kiera. I reached for Kiera's door and jumped back, muttering a curse after touching the doorknob. "Holy hell, Kiera. Is it spelled with literal fire?"

It is, she said telepathically. *But if you still have the dagger I saw you carrying, if it's anything like mine, it should cool it.*

It should? Was there nothing my magic dagger couldn't do?

Give it a try. What do we have to lose?

Taking her at her word, I pressed the tip of the dagger into the lock. Magic flashed brightly and then sputtered out as if it were a dud at a fireworks show.

Do it again! Kiera sounded desperate now.

Determined to make it work, I pressed the dagger against the lock, making sure it touched the knob, too. Lightning bolts of magic crackled around the blade, but still the lock on the door didn't budge.

"Want the key?" someone asked, appearing in the hallway out of nowhere.

I let out a startled cry and jumped back, pressing my hand to my chest to keep my heart from bursting through my ribcage. "Holy fuck. Who are you?"

"The last woman Derek kept locked in that room."

I scanned her, taking in her white flowing dress, long dark hair, and the circles under her eyes. It was only on the second scan that I noticed she was floating above the floor a good twelve to sixteen inches. "You're a ghost."

"Brilliant. Someone give the woman a medal! She

recognized a ghost when she saw one. Big fucking deal. There are ghosts all over this place. How could there not be with that lunatic in charge?"

"Uh, you mentioned a key?" I asked when I finally got my wits back.

"It's downstairs in the drawer next to the dishwasher." She popped back out of existence.

"Do you think the key would work?" I asked Kiera through the door.

It's what Derek uses to get in.

"Kiera?"

Yeah?

"Why are you only speaking to me telepathically?"

It's the only way I can.

I couldn't fathom why that might be the case, but there was no time to question her. I quickly ran downstairs, rummaged through a junk drawer next to the dishwasher, and came up with a set of keys. The correct one had to be on there, right? I hoped like hell that was the case.

Once I was back upstairs, I started trying keys, and the third time was the charm. The key slid in easily, and a second later I heard the lock click.

The door swung open, revealing Kiera standing in the middle of the room, her expression full of hope. But it quickly turned to one of horror as her eyes widened and her lips formed an O with no sound coming out.

Instinct took over. I spun, holding my dagger out in front of me with both hands. Magic poured down on me from seemingly nowhere. It was just a constant stream from somewhere deep within the fabric of space. It was as if a portal of magic had opened up and was ready to obliterate me.

I recalled what Brix had said. The dagger was my tool, and

it would likely save my life. That was for damned sure. Because I wasn't letting some pissed off man-child who used his power and authority to break all kinds of laws win this one.

He'd have to kill me first. But I vowed to go down swinging and take as much from him as I possibly could.

CHAPTER 25

My dagger was powerful, but the magical vortex swirling around me was stronger. My arms were shaking as my body jerked so hard my teeth clanked together. Just holding off the magic wasn't enough. I needed to do something, anything to slow it down. The problem was, I couldn't find its origin.

It felt as if the magic was coming from multiple attack points, and while I'd managed to contain it by holding my dagger in place, that didn't help me much if I wanted to damage the magical portal. If I could just feed the magic back into itself, I was certain I'd have a fighting chance.

I just needed— *Wait... there.* A small opening. Right there in front of me. I held the dagger up with both hands and focused. The chaos around me dissipated, my arms stopped shaking, and I no longer felt like I was going to burst out of my skin.

The power trying to destroy my dagger faltered like there was a sudden glitch in the intensity, and I struck. Using both hands, I brought the dagger down, stabbing the source with everything I had.

Immediately I was blasted into Kiera's room as a magical explosion took place in the hallway. My dagger floated suspended in the air for a few seconds before falling lifelessly to the floor.

I stared at the dagger, unable to believe that I'd done it. That I'd beaten the magical chains that had been holding Kiera hostage. But as reality started to sink in, I turned and rushed toward her, throwing my arms around my friend.

We stood there, hugging tightly for a few moments until I said, "We have to get Kennedy and get out of here."

She nodded once, took my hand, and together we rushed to the door.

"No one's going anywhere," Erikson said, suddenly filling the doorway. He had the hilt of my dagger in one hand and was tapping the blade on his other one.

"Fuck me. Can't I catch even a small break?" I asked the universe.

"Doesn't look like it, Miss Matched. Though if you'd stayed out of this like you were warned, you wouldn't be in this mess right now. It's not like I didn't give you enough warnings. One very explicit one. Stop looking, or I'll destroy everyone around you. Remember that? I think another disaster at your boyfriend's job site is in order. After that, I'll make sure your friend's production never sees the light of day. Then there's your aunt, your father, the coven. So many people to punish on your behalf. Think about that while you're begging for me to set you and your son free."

"Ty?" I cried out, frantic that they'd somehow managed to abduct him, too.

"I thought his name was Bentley or Trinity? Something like that," Erikson said in an unconcerned tone. "Something far too uppity for my operation anyway."

Too uppity? What in the ever-loving shit did that mean? "Kennedy?" I asked.

He snapped his fingers. "That's it. But don't worry. He'll get a new name and eventually he'll be one of us."

"The hell he will," I said, my hands balling into fists. "You'll release him and let him walk out of here unharmed, or you'll have me to contend with."

"Really?" He eyed the dagger. "Somehow, without this, I seriously doubt you even have enough power to keep wielding that sharp tongue of yours."

He waved his hand, sending a bolt of magic in my direction.

I threw my hands up to block the attack, but it was a failed effort. The magic hit me square in the face, nearly knocking me on my ass. I opened my mouth to let out a string of expletives, but nothing came out. I tried again, only to find that I was mute.

"That's better," Erikson said, looking smug. "I always did prefer it when my women didn't talk. It's just so... peaceful."

I charged him, my rage off the charts, but he just slammed the door shut. The sound of the bolt sliding into place made me want to vomit. I grabbed the doorknob and frantically tried to open the door, even though I knew Erikson had locked it.

Laughter filled the hallway along with the sound of retreating footsteps.

I'm sorry, Kiera said.

Me too. I sat down and let my head thunk back against the door. *But at least we can somehow communicate telepathically, right?* I added, trying to find the bright side. Because I really needed one right now.

No. I meant sorry for getting you involved. I never meant for any of this to happen.

I stared at my friend, trying to see all the way down into

her soul. If I could still see auras, what color would hers be? I squinted in her direction and thought I could just make out a faint trace of reddish purple. It was the same as it had always been. Which told me that she hadn't changed at all and was still the same person I'd helped escape a dangerous situation all those years ago. I patted the floor beside me. *I think you need to fill me in on what actually happened that day I picked you up in Utah.*

Kiera nodded once and gingerly lowered herself to the floor to sit next to me. *Derek is my husband,* she said.

So you were leaving an abusive relationship, I confirmed.

She nodded. *But it's worse than that. Two years into our marriage, I found out he's the ringleader of a sophisticated criminal network. He has minions who work for him, stealing things, selling drugs, running scams, pretty much doing anything to make a quick buck. But worst of all, they don't hesitate to eliminate people who get in their way.*

Is it true you're a former Magical Task Force agent?

She nodded once.

And so is Derek's brother, Brix?

Kiera frowned. *Derek's brother's name is Brian. But yes, he was an agent. He disappeared seven years ago. About a month before I ran, I found out he learned the truth about Derek and was going to turn him in, but Derek got trumped up charges filed against him. He lost everything. His fiancée, his job, his family. Just like me.*

Is that why you ran, too? Did your husband set you up for manslaughter charges?

Tears ran down her face as she nodded her head slowly.

My heart nearly shattered in two as I watched her try desperately to pull herself together.

It was my best friend's husband. Derek shot him in the chest, then shot her in the abdomen. She was pregnant. She and her husband survived. *The baby didn't. He used a memory spell to make them think it was me instead of him. To my knowledge, they still think it was me that shot them.*

And that bastard pinned that on you?

He said it was to help me learn my lesson. Piece of shit. He's the one who belongs behind bars. Only that will never happen, because he's the Magical Task Force's golden god. They'd do anything for him since he solves all the cases. It's too bad they don't realize over fifty percent of them are cover-ups and another twenty-five percent always go unsolved. It's hard to have a case without any evidence. He's good at destroying anything that might lead to him.

Including you and me? I asked.

Especially you and me." She turned to look me in the eye. *Make no mistake, Marion. If there is one thing Derek Erikson cannot stand, it's being outmaneuvered by a woman. That's what we did starting that day back in Utah. And he'll destroy us both for it.*

CHAPTER 26

*I*t seemed like hours went by as Kiera and I sat in that room against the door. My mind was racing. I still had so many questions. But I also couldn't stop thinking about escape plans. Because I wasn't going to let a douche like Derek Erikson get the better of me.

There's one thing I don't understand, I said suddenly.

Kiera turned to look at me, waiting expectantly.

If you're married to Derek, how were you going to marry Garrison? Is that why you went to see him that day? To get a divorce?

I didn't go to see him at all, she said. *I was supposed to be meeting someone else who was going to finalize my divorce so that I'd be free of Derek for good. At the last minute, I got a really bad feeling about things and decided to leave any traces of Garrison behind just in case. I didn't want anything traced back to him, but I failed. Derek knows everything. He set me up and then started terrorizing you and everyone around you to get you to leave it alone.* Her eyes filled with tears and she didn't bother to try to stop them this time. *He almost succeeded, too, right? It wasn't until Vince fucked up and abducted Kennedy that you ended up here.*

That's true. He did succeed. I reached out and grabbed her hand, holding it tightly. *I really didn't know what to believe. But then Kennedy was taken and Brix showed up...* I stopped communicating as I thought of Brix. What had happened to him? Had Derek killed his own brother. My stomach turned just thinking about it.

Brix, Kiera asked. *You mentioned him before. You think Brix is Brian, Derek's brother?*

I nodded.

She blew out a breath. *Then there's still hope.*

I didn't have the heart to tell her otherwise.

WHEN THE SUN ROSE, I was wide awake, standing at the window and looking out over the wooded countryside. Erikson had chosen his lair well. There wasn't anything else around. No one would find this road unless they knew what they were looking for. Thinking that help was on the way was a fool's errand.

The only way out of this mess was to rely on each other.

You were a Magical Task Force agent, right? I asked Kiera.

Yes.

You must still have some magic, then. Like Erikson? I have some, too. I demonstrated by letting the magic curl at my fingertips, but then quickly squashed it when I felt my energy rapidly draining. *If we combine our magic, we might just get somewhere.*

Interest briefly lit the other woman's gaze but quickly vanished. *He's way too strong. It'll only make things worse for us. Or worse for those we love.*

Son of a... I hadn't even thought about him going after my loved ones now. He had me. Why did he have to bother with them? But I supposed Kiera was right. If I suddenly became a pain in the ass, he wouldn't hesitate to punish me that way. He already knew it worked. In fact, it might be the only thing that worked.

What's the plan, then? Just sit here and wait for him to let us rot? Or force us into his gang of dipshits? I asked.

She just shook her head and I got the feeling that she'd resigned herself to her fate the moment Erikson had taken possession of my dagger. Well, that wasn't going to work for me. If there was an opening, I'd take it.

TWO ENTIRE DAYS went by without anyone even checking on us. We ate granola bars that had been left in the room and drank water from the adjoining bathroom. By the beginning of the third day, I was ready to torch the place to the ground if it meant I could get out of that room. I was standing by that window, staring at nothing when I heard it. The faint crunch of tires on dirt. Not just one vehicle, there had to be two, maybe even three.

Erikson has visitors, I said.

Kiera didn't respond. She just moved to stand next to me.

We were silent as we listened to the slam of car doors and then the unmistakable thud of boots on the porch.

This was it. This was my chance. With any luck, at least one of them would've left the key in their vehicle and then Kiera and I could make a getaway. My only hesitation was that Kennedy could still be there. But I was no use to him if I was weaponless. It was far better to get away and then come back with reinforcements.

There were only two ways out of that room. Through the

door or the window. I'd thought long and hard about it, and there was no doubt that the window was our best chance. If I could drop to the porch without breaking a leg, I could make a run for it.

There wasn't much in the room, but there was a small wooden chair with spindly legs. It was the best I was gonna get. I grabbed the chair, walked up to the window, and heaved the chair as hard as I could at the glass. It bounced off, but not before a small crack formed. Progress.

Marion, what the hell? Kiera cried in my head.

I'm getting out of here. You're welcome to join me if you want. I stepped back and smashed the chair against the window again. This time the legs went right through. Encouraged, I repeated my effort and was rewarded when the majority of the glass fell to the porch.

"Jesus fucking Christ! What are you doing?" Erikson cried as he stared up at me.

That tingle in my spine flared to life, and instead of gingerly trying to get down from the second story, I threw myself out of the window, straight at Erikson. I hit my target dead on, flattening him.

Magic crawled all over my body and in that moment, I knew I wouldn't be going back into the makeshift prison. I'd get free or die fighting.

"Get off me, you crazy bitch!" Erikson ordered while trying to ram his palm into my nose.

I twisted, avoiding his blow, while landing one of my own to his groin.

"Motherfucking shit." He curled into himself just like I wanted him to, and I continued my assault on him.

I elbowed him, jabbed him in the eyes, broke his nose, and then kneed him in the balls one more time for good measure before I was hauled off him by a pair of strong arms. I had no idea who the person was, but they got no mercy from me. I send an elbow straight back to the gut and then the other one to his eye socket.

My assailant dropped me and suddenly I was free. I quickly glanced up to see Kiera was gone from the window. I could only hope that she'd escaped and was already on her way to one of the vehicles.

I'd just started running in that direction when Erikson's hand shot out and caught my ankle, sending me head first into the dirt. I grunted, but no sound came out. The only thing to do was to fight. And fight dirty.

He released my ankle and tried to scramble to his feet, but I swept his leg, thwarting his efforts. I jumped on him, and the magic still coursing through me made me feel twenty-times stronger than I had before. My fists flew at his chest, pounding over and over again, sending my chaotic magic skirting all over him. If he didn't end up with a bunch of bruises, I'd be surprised.

"Get the fuck off me," Erikson growled and found the leverage to roll us over. He had one of my hands pinned but couldn't control both. I used my free hand to clobber him in the eye and then punch him in the kidney.

"Shit!" He rolled off me, and that's when I saw it. My dagger. He had it strapped to his belt and had been carrying it around like it was his.

Over my dead body. I quickly reached down and grabbed it. The blade turned so blue it nearly blinded me.

But not Erikson. His hand shot up and grabbed my wrist, nearly making me drop it just from the pain.

"Fuck off, Erikson. You'll never get this out of my hands

again," I warned and then clamped my mouth shut. Where had the words come from?

The dagger.

That's what it was. With my magical weapon in my possession, I was able to break Erikson's shitty curse.

The task force agent got to his feet and crouched down into a defensive position, holding his hands out as he said, "Let's do it then."

If it hadn't been such a serious situation, it might have been laughable. How ridiculous was it that a grown man was acting like we were in a cage fight? Though for all intents and purposes, I supposed we were. Only one of us was going to walk away from this. "Let's go, asshole."

He lunged at me, but I was too quick. I spun out of his range and came back in with my dagger ready. One jab and the blade sliced his forearm. Erikson glanced at it in disgust and then redoubled his efforts.

I jabbed again, but this time it was a fake and I came back with a punch to the nose.

Someone behind us let out a groan of sympathy. "Damn, that's got to hurt."

Ignoring our spectator, I kicked out, only to be blocked and struck by a blow to the gut. I was winded for just a moment and suffered from my inability to get the hell out of his striking range. Two more blows landed. One to my head and the other to my chest.

Move! I ordered myself and staggered back, narrowly avoiding a broken nose.

We circled each other a few more rounds, each of us taking our hits. Though because I had the dagger and Erikson didn't, he was sporting a lot more blood.

"Are you ready for this to be over, Marion?" Erikson snarled.

"As ready as you are," I replied.

"Good." He nodded once.

Two sets of arms grabbed me from behind, holding me in place while Erikson walked up to me, his lips curled into a nasty grin. "You've had your fun. Now It's time for me to finish this. He held his hand out to one of his henchmen. "Hand me my knife."

A switchblade was placed into his palm, and all I could think about was the possibility that I was going to be gutted like a pig. No effing way.

"Drop the dagger and things will go smoother for you."

"Nice try. But that's not happening," I said, keeping my voice calm, trying not to portray the fact that my blood had run cold. I still had my dagger and the magic was still right at my fingertips, but that wasn't super helpful when I was being held down by two burly men who had my arms in human vice grips.

"Then I'll be happy to take it from you." Erikson raised the switchblade, ready to strike.

"No!" Kiera cried, her voice raspy as she flew at him, a dagger in both hands.

He turned, his eyes wide with shock before he recovered and took up that same stupid defensive stance he'd had with me.

The vice grips holding my arms must have gotten distracted, because suddenly there was a little movement in their grips. I took full advantage by quickly stomping on both of their insteps, yanking myself free, and then throwing two punches to lay them out flat. With my goons preoccupied, I watched as Kiera and Erikson battled.

Magic was crawling all over one of the daggers Kiera held, and I remembered the one Hollister and I had found on the side of the road. Had she gotten it back? Was that why she was suddenly speaking again, too? If so, how had she recovered it?

"I told Derek you were trouble and that we'd be better off putting you in the ground right away," a man said from behind me.

I spun to find Vince scowling at me. "Where's Kennedy?"

"He's… tied up." The snicker he added to that answer led me to believe that Kennedy wasn't just busy. He was actually tied up somewhere.

"You can fuck all the way off, Vince."

He scowled and charged. I stepped aside and found myself face to face with Hollister.

"Hollister!" I cried. "You're here."

Without a word, he handed me a second dagger and together, we neutralized Vince and then moved to help Kiera. We surrounded Erikson, intending to box him in, but before we could do anything more, Kiera let out a loud battle cry and plunged her dagger into his chest.

Erikson's eyes nearly popped out while his entire body vibrated from the magic still pulsing through the dagger.

Kiera stood in front of him, her expression blank. "You're done tormenting people now, Derek. Do you understand?"

The task force agent didn't answer her. He was trapped in his own web while all his power was drained from him. Finally, after what seemed like hours, he collapsed at her feet. Kiera stared down at him before giving him one last swift kick in the balls. His limp body didn't even flinch.

We all stood together, none of us moving for a long moment, and then I stuffed my daggers into one hand and pulled Kiera into a fierce hug. "It's over," I whispered to her. "It's done."

Her entire body trembled as tears soaked my shirt.

"It's okay, Kiera. Garrison is waiting for you," Hollister said, gently prying her from my arms and engulfing her. He nodded in the direction of the parking lot, and it was there that I spotted Jax and Kennedy.

Kennedy wore dirty, tattered clothes, but he was whole and he was safe.

My heart soared, and I ran, flinging myself at Kennedy. We grasped onto each other, both of us silent. There wasn't anything to say. Not yet. All that mattered was that we were safe.

Finally, he released me and said, "I'll be in Jax's truck."

I brushed a lock of hair out of his eyes. "We'll be right there."

Once Kennedy was gone, Jax caught me around the middle and spun me around, whispering how much he'd missed me, how proud he was, and for me to promise to never leave him like that again.

I pulled back just enough to meet his eyes. "I promise."

CHAPTER 27

*I*n the days after the take down of Agent Erikson, Brix, Kiera, and I spent a lot of time answering questions for the Magical Task Force. It turned out that Brix had spent years gathering evidence against his brother to clear both his and Kiera's names, and within days, all charges against them both were dropped.

More than a dozen people who'd worked with Erikson were arrested after one of them turned on the others to cut a plea deal. Vince had gone to jail, while Erikson had died at the scene. But because of the abundance of witnesses, there was only a cursory investigation into his death. It turned out that when he abducted multiple people, no one much cared when he got what was coming to him.

It had taken a while to get the full story of why Kiera and I had been left at Erikson's house for days before Brix, Jax, and Hollister had arrived. Erikson had come close to killing Brix. In fact, Erikson had probably thought he'd delivered a fatal blow to his brother's neck, but thanks to Brix's healer powers, he'd been able to close the wound just enough to survive until he'd found someone stronger and more skilled at healing punctured arteries. He almost hadn't made it.

It had taken three days to heal, but by then, he'd already tracked down Hollister and Jax and had gotten both to agree to be his backup when he came back for us. To hear Jax tell it, Brix had come in full throttle, taking down anyone in his path. Hollister had been right behind him, ready to arm Kiera with her dagger the moment he had a chance. Jax had been backup muscle to make sure no one surprised them.

They all said the highlight of the rescue was when I jumped out the window and flattened Erikson. I had to admit that I wished we'd gotten that on video. If I could have uploaded that to Instagram, no doubt I'd finally go viral for something that didn't make me look like a fool... like that unfortunate incident when the internet had found out I was dating Jax after I'd set him up on a date with Lennon Love. In the end, it had all worked out, but in that moment... yeah. I planned to do whatever it took to avoid any public faux pas from now until eternity.

It was early morning and I was sitting on my front porch, wrapped in a blanket, sipping a cup of coffee when Ty appeared in front of me with his own cup in hand.

"Morning," he said.

I smiled up at him. "Morning. Did you have a good night?"

He took the seat next to me, and when he wrapped his arms around himself, I offered him part of my blanket. He gladly accepted and then closed his eyes as he took a long sip from his mug. "Last night was... interesting."

I raised my eyebrows, not quite sure I wanted to hear the rest. He'd come straight home when he'd heard Kennedy and I had been abducted. But after a few days, we'd both insisted that he go back and finish the job he'd started. Now that the project had ended, he was back for an undisclosed time and he and Kennedy were trying to work out their relationship. "I noticed Kennedy slept in his room last night. That doesn't seem like what you were hoping for."

Ty chuckled softly. "Moms. They really are clueless, aren't they?"

"You're calling me clueless? Me? Did you know the Magical Task Force is trying to recruit me? After everything that went down, they said they're looking for talented people with integrity. It doesn't sound like they think I'm clueless." While the offer with the Magical Task Force was tempting, I kept turning them down. I wasn't really all that interested in fighting bad guys. I just wanted to build my matching making business, and spend some time understanding the extent of my new powers that the dagger brought me. Maybe in the future when I had more experience, I'd consider helping the agency out. Until then, I was happy to focus on work and family.

He smirked. "I meant about where Kennedy slept last night. Do you sleep like the dead or something? We weren't exactly quiet when I came inside after he went to bed and dragged him back out."

"Oh. Was that you and Kennedy talking? I was sort of... distracted."

That got a snort out of him. "I suppose a hot contractor guy will do that to you."

"You'd suppose correctly." I eyed the young man next to me. "So, I take it the two of you worked some issues out then?"

He shrugged one shoulder. "Something like that. We're definitely still dating, and he says he's ready to move back into the garage apartment. Kennedy also said he'd come and spend time with me down in LA during my next project. Skyler has work for him down there to help with a satellite store they're opening shortly."

"That's great." I reached over and squeezed his hand. "I'm really happy for you both. Does this mean you'll be leaving soon to go back to work?"

"Not soon." He squeezed my hand this time. "I want to spend some time with my Mama Marion."

I chuckled. "You know you don't have to do that. I'm fine. Really."

"You might be, but I'm not sure I am." All his humor was gone. "Nothing matters more to me than family. That's what I told Kennedy last night, and now I'm telling you. You're my family, Marion. If anything ever happened to you or Kennedy..." He shook his head. "No sound job is more important than either of you."

"Of course not," I said gently. "But that doesn't mean you don't follow your dreams. Both of us support you in that, you know."

His last job had been a little rocky when Erikson was meddling, but afterward when Erikson's corruption had been exposed, the project had been all smooth sailing. The same had occurred for Tandy's production, and once Jax and his crew got back on track, the build had come in only a week late. It appeared all the crazy drama that stemmed from Premonition Pointe had settled for the moment at least.

"I know you do," Ty said. "That goes both ways, right? I can be here for a while to support you, too. Kennedy and I need some time together, and as sweet as it is that he says he'll come to LA, I know he's not ready to leave you yet. So we've decided to spend some time helping you out here. I know you have a bunch of upgrades you want to do to the house. Make a list and Kennedy and I will tackle what we can. If there's anything outside of our skillset, we'll consult Jax."

"You don't have to do any of that," I insisted.

He grinned. "That's the beauty of it. We know we don't have to. We want to."

My eyes stung with tears. The happy kind. I reached over and pulled him into a one-armed hug. "I love you. You know that right?"

"Yeah," he said, sounding choked up. "Just want you to know that I'd go to the ends of the earth to find *your* boyfriend if he ever goes missing, too."

"Bite your tongue," I said without any heat. "And I know you would. But let's pray to the goddess that you never have to do that."

"Gladly," he said, and when he pulled away, he had to wipe at his eyes, too.

When Ty got up to head back to the garage apartment, I called after him, "Don't forget about dinner tonight with Dad and Aunt Lucy. They both say they have news."

"Kennedy and I wouldn't miss it," he called back.

The door to the apartment opened, and Kennedy stuck his head out. Their little pup, Paris Francine, ran around at his feet, nipping and biting at his toes. Kennedy picked her up, kissed her on her head, and then grinned at me. "Morning, Marion."

"Morning," I called back.

As Kennedy placed the puppy back into the apartment, Ty took the stairs two at a time, and when he got to the top, Kennedy wrapped his arm around his neck, kissed him, and hastily pulled him inside.

I couldn't help the smile that tugged at my lips. Nothing made me more pleased than seeing the two of them happy.

Twenty minutes later, I was still enjoying the cool morning breeze when a black BMW pulled into my driveway. Hollister jumped out and ran over to take the seat Ty had been using.

"You're out early," I said. "What brings you by before breakfast?"

"It's nearly eight, Marion," he said with a chuckle.

"Yeah. That's early for a Sunday."

"I'm headed back home today. I wanted to stop by and say goodbye."

That surprised me. Hollister had been working with the Magical Task Force agency for weeks now, helping them upgrade their weapons and spells they used in combat. It had turned out that he was one of the only people who knew how to neutralize all of the potions and spelled objects that Erikson had been stockpiling. After decommissioning a warehouse of inventory, he'd made specific items for the remaining agents that would complement their skills rather than being a one-size-fits-all situation.

"I'm sorry to see you go," I said honestly. Hollister had become a good friend during the time he'd been in Premonition Pointe. "We'll miss you."

"I'll miss investigating with you, Marion. I don't think I've ever met anyone quite as fearless as you."

I scoffed. "Oh, I have plenty of fear. I just have a lot more righteous indignation that fuels my irrational side."

"That's fair." He paused for a second and then added, "I also want to apologize for the things I said when I left town last time. I had no right to judge you for your decision to stop looking for Kiera. With the information we had—"

"Stop," I said. "There's no need to apologize. We should've never stopped looking. That's one thing I learned from you.

When you know in your gut what's right, you follow your gut. I would have, too, if I hadn't been so scared."

"I know. That's the reason for the apology."

Silence fell between us. It always did when someone brought up the time when Kiera was on her own. I wasn't sure I'd ever get over the guilt. I cleared my throat. "How are Garrison and Kiera doing?"

Hollister grinned. "Perfect. Garrison's done with his cancer treatments and Kiera is back to work at her graphic design business. You know the Magical Task Force is heavily recruiting her to come back, right? They thought Brix could convince her."

It hadn't taken the powers that be at the agency to bring Brix back into the fold. He'd only agreed if they gave him a big promotion with his own department. After everything that went down, they'd been eager to appease him. Now he was a big shot who handpicked the cases he wanted to work on.

"I didn't know that, but I guess I'm not surprised. I take it she isn't interested?" I'd be shocked if she went back to the organization that had completely failed her. But now that Erikson was gone, I guessed it was a possibility.

"No. She said she might consult on special cases, but as far as having a career there, she's not interested. She likes her life. Lots of time to be creative with her graphics, spend time with Garrison, and help me and Garrison develop more products in the store."

"That sounds lovely," I said, my heart full. Kiera and Garrison had been through so much. They deserved to live a stress-free life, doing whatever they wanted to do.

"Did you get the scoop on the ménage thrupple?" Celia asked as she popped into existence.

I didn't even flinch. I was so used to her coming and going

when she pleased, I just always expected it. Though she didn't always start off asking about ménage or thrupples. "I didn't," I said and turned to Hollister. "Did you?"

He laughed. "There's no thrupple or ménage going on at the office with the director. Or if there is, no one is admitting to it. The general consensus is that it was a planted rumor so you'd have something to focus on other than the real-life corruption that was going on under everyone's noses."

"Well, that's boring as shit," Celia said, waving a hand. "And to think I skipped out of bed early for this non-gossip. I'm out. Maybe I can—"

"Celia Marie!" a man's voice boomed from the ether. "Get back here right now, or I swear to the goddess above, no more hanky panky for you."

"Hanky panky?" I asked.

Celia glanced down at her feet, and I'd swear if a ghost could blush, she'd have been bright red. "Danny doesn't like it when I leave before we finish our... morning romp. Gotta go!"

The ghost vanished, leaving Hollister and I chuckling at her shenanigans.

CHAPTER 28

"*A* toast to Aunt Lucy and Gael. Maybe your trip around the world will be everything you dream of," Tazia said, holding up a champagne glass.

Jax was the first to hold his glass up, and we all followed.

The lot of us said, "To Lucy and Gael!"

Aunt Lucy leaned into her Brendon Urie look-alike boyfriend and flushed.

I hid a giggle, knowing exactly what she was thinking.

Her boyfriend, Gael, stood up and raised his own glass. "I'd like to toast to Marion. If it wasn't for her, I'd have never met this fabulous creature, and I certainly wouldn't be cruising to Greece. So thank you, Marion, you're the best damned matchmaker to ever set foot this side of the Mississippi."

"You mean there are better ones east of the great river?" I teased, smiling up at him. Gael had turned out to not only be great fun for my aunt, but he was also the sweetest man I'd ever met. I couldn't think of a better match for Lucy. She deserved the best, and Gael was certainly hitting the mark. "Thank you, Gael. I just want my aunt to be happy. So take care of her and don't let any Greek gods steal her away. We'd miss her too much."

"You can bet your life on that. This one isn't getting away from me." He draped his arm over her shoulders and leaned in to kiss her temple. It was all just so cute; I wasn't sure how I was going to handle it.

"If we're giving toasts," my dad said, rising from his chair, "I have one, too."

We all gave our attention to my father. Memphis Matched wasn't one to make a fuss about things, so a toast for him was a big deal.

"Just so you know," Jax whispered in my ear. "I won't be standing up in front of everyone declaring my intentions. I'll make them perfectly clear later."

I stifled a chuckle, trying to look innocent as my father sent us a sharp look.

Dad cleared his throat and held out a hand to Tazia.

She glanced around nervously but let him pull her up to stand by him. "What's going on, Memphis?"

"I just wanted to make a toast to you, the loveliest lady I've ever had the pleasure to spend time with. And while we're at it..." He paused for dramatic effect, and I nearly stopped breathing.

Was he going to do what I thought he was going to do? If the man got down on one knee, I was certain I'd die from heart failure. After all these years of running from love, if he—

"Tazia, we've been dancing around this for weeks," my father said, his cheeks flushing. "I just wanted to ask you if we could make it official?"

This was it. He was going to ask her. I glanced at Jax, who was sitting next to me, and gave him a wide-eyed *holy shit* look. He gave me an amused smile.

"Make what official, Memphis?" Tazia asked nervously.

He frowned. "Us. This." He waved his hand between them. "You know, go steady."

"Oh. My. Gods," I muttered under my breath.

"I heard that Marion. What would you call it? Exclusively dating?" my father asked me.

I cleared my throat. "Going steady seems appropriate," I said, hiding my chuckle. My poor father. He was so commitment averse, but here he was, asking Tazia to take a chance on him in front of his entire family. Whether she knew it or not, this was a huge deal.

Tazia seemed to understand how important this was to my dad, because she wrapped her arm around his waist, leaned in, and kissed him softly before saying, "I'd be honored to go steady. Do I get a class pin?"

He whispered something in her ear that made her giggle, and even though I was certain it was something dirty, I didn't care. Not in the least bit. Everyone I loved best was at my table, happy and safe and full of love. It was just about as perfect as life could get.

Ding Dong.

"Who could that be?" Ty asked, looking around the table. "Did you invite someone else, Marion?"

"Nope. I'll get it." I got up, musing on who could be stopping by. All the coven members knew I was hosting a family dinner. As far as I knew, they all had their own plans. I supposed it could be Iris, but she would've called. Maybe just a solicitor.

I opened the door, ready to tell whoever was on the other side that we weren't interested, but instead, I found myself staring at a younger woman holding two duffle bags and a small pet carrier.

"Hi, Marion. Surprise!"

I gaped at the tall redhead with too much cleavage and too much red lipstick. "Charlotte?"

"Hey, sis. Long time no talk. Aren't you going to let me in?"

"Well, we're kind of in the middle of a family dinner," I said awkwardly.

"Then I'm here right on time, aren't I?" My estranged half sister, whom I hadn't spoken to in over ten years, pushed her way past me and into my sanctuary.

I followed her and stood back when she said, "Hi, Dad. Miss me?"

All of Dad's good cheer vanished as he took in the woman he was in no way related to but had treated like a daughter for ten years before she'd packed up and left in the middle of the night without even leaving a note. "Charlotte. It's been a long time."

She gave him a wide smile, but from my vantage point, I couldn't help but notice the wobble. "It has." She turned back to me. "Marion, I was hoping Minx and I could crash here for a bit. Just until I can find a place of my own."

The dog in the carrier gave a sad little whine, and even though every molecule in my body was screaming for me to say no, what came out was, "Of course, Charlotte. I'm sure we can make up the guest room for you."

"Thank you." She put the carrier down and wrapped her arms around me. Then she whispered, "I could also use a little help with the curse I just accidentally unleashed on the men down at Hallucinations."

"What?" I asked, but she was already moving toward the bathroom.

"I've got to use the little girl's room. When I'm done, we'll catch up." She waggled her fingers at me and then locked herself in the bathroom.

I turned and stared at my father.

He took a deep breath and said, "I wonder what trouble she'll bring this time."

DEANNA'S BOOK LIST

Witches of Keating Hollow:
Soul of the Witch
Heart of the Witch
Spirit of the Witch
Dreams of the Witch
Courage of the Witch
Love of the Witch
Power of the Witch
Essence of the Witch
Muse of the Witch
Vision of the Witch
Waking of the Witch
Honor of the Witch
Promise of the Witch

Witches of Christmas Grove:
A Witch For Mr. Holiday
A Witch For Mr. Christmas
A Witch For Mr. Winter

A Witch For Mr. Mistletoe

Premonition Pointe Novels:
Witching For Grace
Witching For Hope
Witching For Joy
Witching For Clarity
Witching For Moxie
Witching For Kismet

Miss Matched Midlife Dating Agency:
Star-crossed Witch
Honor-bound Witch
Outmatched Witch

Jade Calhoun Novels:
Haunted on Bourbon Street
Witches of Bourbon Street
Demons of Bourbon Street
Angels of Bourbon Street
Shadows of Bourbon Street
Incubus of Bourbon Street
Bewitched on Bourbon Street
Hexed on Bourbon Street
Dragons of Bourbon Street

Pyper Rayne Novels:
Spirits, Stilettos, and a Silver Bustier
Spirits, Rock Stars, and a Midnight Chocolate Bar
Spirits, Beignets, and a Bayou Biker Gang
Spirits, Diamonds, and a Drive-thru Daiquiri Stand
Spirits, Spells, and Wedding Bells

Ida May Chronicles:
Witched To Death
Witch, Please
Stop Your Witchin'

Crescent City Fae Novels:
Influential Magic
Irresistible Magic
Intoxicating Magic

Last Witch Standing:
Bewitched by Moonlight
Soulless at Sunset
Bloodlust By Midnight
Bitten At Daybreak

Witch Island Brides:
The Wolf's New Year Bride
The Vampire's Last Dance
The Warlock's Enchanted Kiss
The Shifter's First Bite

Destiny Novels:
Defining Destiny
Accepting Fate

Wolves of the Rising Sun:
Jace
Aiden
Luc
Craved
Silas

Darien
Wren

Black Bear Outlaws:
Cyrus
Chase
Cole

Bayou Springs Alien Mail Order Brides:
Zeke
Gunn
Echo

ABOUT THE AUTHOR

New York Times and USA Today bestselling author, Deanna Chase, is a native Californian, transplanted to the slower paced lifestyle of southeastern Louisiana. When she isn't writing, she is often goofing off with her husband in New Orleans or playing with her two shih tzu dogs. For more information and updates on newest releases visit her website at deannachase.com.

Made in United States
North Haven, CT
29 November 2022

27546917R00148